smart novels
U.S. HISTORY

Shades of Blue and Gray

Volume II

by Lynne Hansen

SPARK**NOTES**

Spark Publishing
A Division of Barnes & Noble
120 Fifth Avenue
New York, NY 10011
www.sparknotes.com

ISBN-13: 978-1-4114-9674-3
ISBN-10: 1-4114-9674-4

Library of Congress Cataloging-in-Publication Data

Hansen, Lynne, 1968–
  Shades of blue and gray / by Lynne Hansen.
    p. cm.—(Smart Novels)
  Summary: Twenty-first-century teenager Mindy Gold accompanies twenty-second-century "time-cop" Jasper Gordon to the Battle of Bull Run in 1861 Virginia to search for seventeenth-century minister Jonathan Hartthorne; Chad, the cutest boy in Mindy's high school; and Andros, their alien captor.
  ISBN-13: 978-1-4114-9674-3 (pbk.: alk. paper)
  ISBN-10: 1-4114-9674-4 (pbk.: alk. paper)
  [1. Time travel—Fiction. 2. Bull Run, 1st Battle of, Va., 1861—Fiction. 3. Extraterrestrial beings—Fiction. 4. Virginia—History—Civil War, 1861–1865—Fiction. 5. United States—History—Civil War, 1861–1865—Fiction. 6. Science fiction.] I. Title.

PZ7.H198252Sha 2007
[Fic]—dc22

                                                                    2007021150

Please submit changes or report errors to www.sparknotes.com/errors.

Printed and bound in the United States

10 9 8 7 6 5 4 3 2 1

CONTENTS

FROM THE CHRONOLYZER'S HARD DRIVE:

The Story So Far . . .

In *A Time for Witches,* Mindy Gold is sent back in time by a device called a *chronobomb* detonated by a mysterious being named Andros. Mindy's sister Serena and several of her classmates are also within range of the blast, and each of them is sent back to a different time and place in American history. Finding herself in 1692 Salem at the height of the Salem Witch Trial hysteria, Mindy is approached by Jasper Gordon, a time-cop from the future. Jasper explains that Andros is the agent of the Galagians, an alien race of time travelers who can possess the bodies of human beings. Andros's chronobomb not only sent Mindy and her friends back in time, but it also created pathways for the Galagians to enter the human time stream. Jasper enlists Mindy's help in finding her friends and sending them back to their own time while expelling the Galagians from the humans they have taken possession of.

Mindy and Jasper are quickly arrested by the Salem authorities on suspicion of witchcraft, and the only person willing to aid them is Jonathan Hartthorne, a nineteen-year-old Puritan minister and naturalist. When Mindy and Jasper finally use Jasper's chronolyzer to escape to the future, they unwittingly take the young minister with them.

Now, Mindy and Jasper must travel to the Civil War Battle of Bull Run, in search of Mindy's classmate (and former crush) Chad. Unfortunately, Andros hijacks Jonathan Hartthorne's body and goes there first . . .

CHARACTERS

Mindy Gold. A seventeen-year-old girl from modern-day Salem, Massachusetts.

Serena Gold. Mindy's younger sister, who is sent back in time at the same time as Mindy, but to a different time and place. Current whereabouts unknown.

Jasper Gordon. A young time-policeman from the twenty-sixth century. The chronopolice possess powerful technology and serve a totalitarian state in the future. There seems to be more to Jasper than meets the eye, though, as he often operates outside of Future State protocols.

Jonathan Hartthorne. A nineteen-year-old minister from colonial Salem, accidentally brought with Jasper and Mindy into the future.

The chronolyzer. A sentient, handheld communication and information device. The chronolyzer can transport you in time, provide you with appropriate period costumes, and tell you whatever you need to know about the period you're in—but with an obnoxious attitude.

Andros. A mysterious being working for the Galagians. Whether Andros is a Galagian or something else is unclear. Andros can time-travel and take possession of people's bodies.

The Galagians. Aliens who exist outside of time, and who seek human bodies to inhabit. They can only possess humans who have tempose in their blood, a substance that most humans produce in the future, but few or none do in the past. Unfortunately, Andros can make humans in the past habitable to the aliens.

Chapter One

As Mindy Gold whirled through the time stream, she discovered time travel wasn't any less disorienting the third time around than it had been the first two times. Her only consolation was that although she wasn't from 2512 herself, at least she'd been there before. After spending several days in 1692 Salem during the infamous witch trials, and even getting accused of being a witch herself, Mindy was looking forward to something familiar and normal.

She wasn't going to get it.

The white plasticite Safe Room in the transportation hub of the Time Stream Investigation headquarters smelled of antiseptic and vanilla extract. The surface she was lying on felt bumpy—firm yet pliant.

Mindy Gold opened her eyes. She had arrived in 2512 sprawled awkwardly on top of the very buff, very naked Puritan minister Jonathan Hartthorne. He lay on top of a chrome examination table, unconscious.

Mindy scrambled off of him so quickly she couldn't keep her feet beneath her and ended up on her butt on the cold white tile floor, her head at just the right height to give her an even better vantage point for viewing his nakedness. She blushed and scooted away.

Jasper Gordon, the slender, pixie-ish Time Stream Investigator who'd brought her into the future, leaned over her, amused.

"Sure and if you could tear your eyes away from the reverend's privates for five seconds and lend me your full attention, I'd be much obliged, Mindy Gold." Jasper spoke in a rich, lilting Irish brogue.

"Not funny, Jasper."

"Right, well your landing on him wasn't my doing." He held up his chronolyzer, a palm-sized electronic organizer that knew everything and could do just about as much. The screen read, SORRY ABOUT THAT. "When we time-travel, the chronolyzer calculates the destination coordinates. I have nothing to do with it."

As Mindy stood up, she dusted off her jeans and favorite black hoodie. After picking at her silky, thick brown hair and twisting it up in a scrunchy, she tucked her hands in the pockets of her hoodie. "Well, your machine is either less competent than we've been giving it credit for, or it has a wicked sense of humor."

"Actually, you've put your finger on it. Humans learned hundreds of years ago that for a machine to obtain intelligence and true sentience, it needs to have a sense of humor. Thus, the chronolyzer is programmed with one—annoying as it is."

"Maybe it needs an upgrade." She turned away in irritation. The blinding white and chrome room made her feel like she needed sunglasses and a black suit, or that Tommy Lee Jones and Will Smith would walk through the door any minute carrying ray-guns. The room was way retro, like a 1960s vision of the future. A bank of computers and other machinery lined one wall. Another area held a clear plasticite desk and chair. The chrome examination table she had just rolled off of was part of a medical station.

"Don't you think a clothing receiver might be appropriate for the reverend?" Mindy asked. A clothing receiver was a transparent body stocking that allowed the chronolyzer to program period-appropriate clothing for time travelers—a necessary device because clothes couldn't survive time travel. Mindy had been suited in one after her first travel through time.

Mindy paused and remembered why she was there. They'd just traveled from the twenty-first century, where Mindy saw her sister, Serena. The image of her fifteen-year-old little sister's spiritless body lying motionless beneath the pressed-white hospital sheets haunted her. She'd do anything it took to restore her.

That's why she was in 2512 with the Time Stream Investigator. Andros, an agent of the time-traveling aliens called the Galagians, had stolen the spirits of Serena and several other teens and banished them into the past. Mindy and Jasper were going to find their spirits and restore them to their bodies.

"I've been keeping the reverend unconscious since we arrived," Jasper said. "Since I'm just going to send him back to 1692 anyhow, I didn't figure clothing was all that necessary."

"Well, since we're in mixed company, I'm kind of thinking it *is* necessary," Mindy said.

"Just don't look at Holy Joe if it bothers you."

Mindy wished it were that easy.

The minister from Massachusetts had the body of a tawdry romance novel cover model, the kind in which the guy clutches the full-bosomed damsel in distress to his gleaming pecs. Before Mindy had met him in 1692, she'd imagined colonial ministers to be chicken-necked, pencil-thin Ichabod Cranes who stuttered nervously when they spoke. Jonathan Hartthorne couldn't be any more different. He had a commanding voice, an approachable and friendly personality, and above all, the rugged body of a Greek god. She had a hard time keeping her eyes off him.

Jasper cleared his throat. "I *said,* just don't look at him if it bothers you."

Mindy reluctantly looked away. "Does he really have to go back? I mean, he didn't exactly choose to come with us into the future. Maybe we should at least let him choose whether or not he wants to go back."

"No."

"Can't you at least wake him up so I can say goodbye?" Mindy pleaded. *And so I can gaze into those gorgeous green eyes just once more,* she thought.

"Em, no." Jasper fiddled with the chronolyzer again. Mindy watched the minister exhale softly as he slept through his future. Then, almost imperceptibly, there were words.

"Help . . . me . . ." Minister Hartthorne whispered.

"Jasper, Jonathan's awake."

"I'll give him a wee bit more of the sedative to knock him out."

"Help . . . ME . . ." Hartthorne repeated, this time louder.

"No, wait. There's something wrong."

His voice didn't seem right. It seemed harsher, more gravelly. If she hadn't seen his mouth move, Mindy could have sworn it was someone else speaking.

Suddenly the minister's eyelids popped open, his pupils fully dilated. He gasped for air like a long-distance swimmer who had just come up for his last breath. His forehead broke out in a sweat.

"There's something wrong with him!" Mindy shouted.

A cockeyed, eerie grin spread across the minister's face. His voice was strong now, and definitely not his own. "Help me," he said. "Help me kill your friends."

Typecasting:

The 10 Types of Civil War Soldiers

The Union and Confederate armies weren't entirely composed of stoic young men. A variety of colorful types kept camp lively.

Type #1: The "old man" (experienced West Pointer)

West Point's been cranking out military leaders for a long time. Generals on both sides of the Mason-Dixon line during the Civil War, such as Sherman, Beauregard, Grant, Jackson, and Lee, came from there. Most also spent time in the Mexican-American War (1846–1848). All were really good at barking orders.

Type #2: The "shoulder strap" (inexperienced West Pointer)

With so many of the nation's sons getting shot to bits on the battlefield, it wasn't long before both sides started relying on inexperienced junior officers with no other action experience to lead the troops. Some rose to the occasion; some crumbled. Contemptuous enlisted men referred to these greenies as shoulder straps because of the epaulets on their uniforms. One such strapper was recent graduate George Armstrong Custer, who rose to brevet brigadier general for the Union before being filled with arrows by a bunch of Sioux warriors in 1876.

Type #3: The "bumble" (self-important commander)

If you were one of the guys giving the orders, you may have been a bumble. The slang comes from Dickens's *Oliver Twist*, in which Mr. Bumble was the comically corrupt orphan manager. Dickens wasn't a bestselling author among the army rank and file, but the term was known widely enough that it became the moniker for any pompous officer during the war.

Type #4: The "dodger" (thief)

Just because you're willing to fight and die next to somebody doesn't mean you won't steal from him. Dodgers were the usual suspects whenever rations, envelopes, or iPods went missing. Again, the rabble looked to *Oliver Twist* for their clever nickname: "The Artful Dodger" was the nickname of Jack Dawkins, a pickpocket known for his ability to evade the police.

Type #5: The "bummer" (shirker or forager)

German immigrants constituted more than 200,000 of the Union's forces. *Bummler*, their slang word for a shiftless, lazy idler, caught on. It eventually shortened to "bummer," then "bum." It came to stand for the act of getting something for nothing. Nowadays, it can mean both: "Hey, think we can bum a ride from that bum over there?"

Type #6: The "Jonah" (clumsy, unlucky, cursed man)

In the Bible, Jonah's shipmates decide he's bad luck and throw him overboard into the ocean, where he winds up in the belly of a whale. In the Civil War, soldiers took to calling their hapless, unlucky comrades Jonahs.

These were the guys who tripped people up during the march or fell into the cooking fire. Rather than throwing them to the fishes, Civil War–era soldiers just laughed at their Jonahs.

Type #7: The "kid" (buglers and drummers)

Civil War armies were in need of soldiers. Seriously in need. In addition to the youngsters in their late teens and early twenties, both sides put kids as young as thirteen to work as buglers or drummers. In the days before bullhorns and alarm clocks, bugle calls and drum cadences were used to pass along orders. One Union bugler, Tommy Hubler, was only nine when he joined up. But some kids also served in combat, with one ambitious little tot, E. G. Baxter, becoming lieutenant at the ripe old age of thirteen.

Type #8: The "camp follower" (lady of ill repute)

To satisfy certain needs, the men at camp relied on "camp followers." These women would follow both Union and Confederate armies and . . . do their laundry and cook for them. What? What did you think they did? Oh, okay, some would also act as prostitutes.

Type #9: The "puffer" (braggart)

It's often said that war has a way of humbling a man, but that's not always the case. Puffers were braggarts who enjoyed regaling their fellow soldiers with tales of the heroics they pulled off while their mates were getting gunned down and blown up. Puffers were generally tolerated, particularly if their storytelling skills made up for the amount of BS they were dishing out.

Type #10: The "sutler" (guy licensed to make a killing)

Being at war doesn't mean you need to live like a savage. Soldiers still craved the bare essentials, including clean underwear, shaving brushes, medicine, candy, cigars, and whiskey. Sutlers were the traveling merchants contracted to follow the armies around, selling their wares—at huge markups, of course.

Chapter Two

Jasper scanned Minister Hartthorne's body with the chronolyzer. "It's Andros. The little bastard has gotten inside Holy Joe."

"So trap him already," Mindy said. "Suck him out or something."

Still grinning, Minister Hartthorne turned his head toward Mindy but not his body. "I don't think so. I like it here. Nothing more fun than making a man of God misbehave. Besides, look at these pecs!"

Minister Hartthorne jumped down from the chrome table and grabbed Mindy. Pulling her close, he pressed his lips enthusiastically onto hers in a kiss worthy of the romance novel cover model Hartthorne resembled. Stunned, it took Mindy a second to remember to resist. She pounded at his chest.

Andros held her just long enough so that she understood she couldn't get away if he didn't want her to, then released her. "Very nice. I wonder why the stud hasn't done that before. He likes you, you know, but he's trying to be such a good boy." Andros made Minister Hartthorne wink at her.

Mindy backed away just as Jasper came up behind Minister Hartthorne with the plasticite desk chair. Jasper clobbered him over the head with it, but it bounced back and hit the time-cop instead, knocking him backward. The chronolyzer slipped from his pocket and skittered across the slick white tile floor.

"Ah! Just what I need," Andros said, striding toward the chronolyzer.

"Don't let the little fecker get his hands on it," Jasper called. "He'll hop to another time and we'll lose him."

Andros leaned down for the electronic device. Mindy slid and kicked it out of his reach.

He gave an exaggerated pout. "Oh, that wasn't very nice. All I want to do is find my friends . . . just like you."

Jasper scooped up the chronolyzer. "The difference being that when you find your friends, you send Mindy's friends to *Annwfn*— the Void."

Shrugging, Andros said, "And when you find my friends, you banish them back to their mother ship. Same difference."

"You bloody well know being sent to the Void isn't the same as banishment," Jasper said. "It's an eternity as a ghost, a disembodied spirit cursed to a limbo shadow world without a life."

"And just what kind of life does a *human* have anyhow? Most of them can't even time-travel, and how much fun can any existence be if you're relegated to a single physical body?"

"Boring or not," Mindy said, "my friends deserve their lives back. You had no right to blast them into ancient history!"

"They were useful," Andros said. "Probably more useful than they'll ever be in their human lives. How can I explain it so that a mortal mind like yours could possibly understand?" He rubbed Minister Hartthorne's chin, thinking.

Jasper flailed his arms behind Andros's back in what Mindy assumed was a sign for her to keep the alien distracted. "I won't let you kill my friends," Mindy said as Jasper snuck up behind Andros, holding the chronolyzer out like a weapon. *Man, was there anything a chronolyzer couldn't do?* she thought. It was like the Swiss Army knife of electronic devices.

"I think you should know two things," Andros said. "First, I don't care about your friends. Not in the least. I care about *my* friends. And second, you should know that I can feel Jasper's footsteps behind me." Andros whipped around to face the stunned time-cop. With a speed that floored Mindy, Andros snatched the chronolyzer from Jasper's hand.

Jasper leaped at Andros, but his diminutive frame was no match for Minister Hartthorne's chiseled muscles. Andros shrugged off Jasper, tossing him to the ground, where he hit his head on the floor with a bang.

"So long, Mindy-Lou," Andros said, striding for the exit. "Maybe if you find the Rev in the past, he'll kiss you again. You know you want him to." Andros made Minister Hartthorne wink again before he swaggered out the door of the Safe Room.

Mindy raced to the doorway to follow him out, only to be greeted by a blinding flare of light. Andros was gone. Beyond the door was only an empty hallway.

When Mindy returned to the Safe Room, Jasper was sitting up, gingerly touching the back of his head. His fingers came away wet.

"He's gone," Mindy said. "Andros is gone, and he took Minister Hartthorne with him."

"What do you bloody mean, he's fecking gone? This Safe Room has been hermetically sealed in a thick layer of plasticite. It is completely unassailable by all life forms. It is physically impossible that he could be anywhere else but here."

"There is this thing called a door," Mindy said. "You do still call them doors in 2512, don't you?"

Jasper sighed. "Hand me the bastard chronolyzer, would you?"

"He took that too."

Jasper looked like he had swallowed a bug. "Sure and you did hit the alarm to initiate lockdown procedures, though, right?"

"What alarm?"

Jasper pointed at the big red button next to the door labeled ALARM TO INITIATE LOCKDOWN PROCEDURES.

"Uh, no."

Jasper stood up and staggered toward the bank of computers along the far wall, clutching his head. "Cinda, I need a backup chronolyzer sent to Safe Room number 106, immediately."

A chronolyzer slid out of what looked like a vacuum tube in the wall. Jasper grabbed it.

"Chronolyzer, this is Time Stream Investigations Agent Jasper Gordon."

I KNOW WHO YOU ARE, AGENT GORDON, the chronolyzer displayed. ALL TOO WELL, it added.

"So, what—are they all programmed with smart mouths?" Mindy asked.

SMARTER THAN YOU.

"This one's just nasty!" Mindy exclaimed.

I'M THE SAME CHRONOLYZER, DUMMY. MY CONSCIOUSNESS HAS SIMPLY BEEN DOWNLOADED INTO THIS NEW DEVICE.

"Fantastic—so glad to have you back," Mindy quipped. "Anyway, can we get on with this, Jasper? Get the chronolyzer to fix your wound so we can go after Minister Hartthorne." *And Serena,* she thought to herself. But because Andros had only just now made off with the minister's body, she guessed that Jasper would want to stay hot on his trail.

"I'm going after Andros, not Holy Joe," Jasper said as the chronolyzer spat out a clear plastic square. Jasper placed the square on his cut forehead, wincing slightly.

"They're in the same body, so what's the difference?"

"The difference is, wherever Andros goes in the past, the first thing he's likely to do is jump from the Rev into someone new to throw us off his trail."

"So we'd better move fast, or Jonathan is likely to find himself in big trouble."

"*We're* not going anywhere—not with Andros larking about. *You're* staying right here in this Safe Room, Mindy Gold."

"Because we saw how safe it was just now?" Mindy said.

You're wasting time, the chronolyzer typed. I'm authorizing travel for the twenty-first-century teenager, despite her obvious ineptitude.

"*My* ineptitude?"

"But—" Jasper protested.

Prepare for immediate departure.

The world swirled around Mindy, not so much in colors, but in tastes and smells, as if history were a buffet line instead of a timeline. Pumpkin pies burning, cotton candy spinning, frog legs roasting, yeast bubbling. The weightlessness of time travel ended as she landed hard on her back, the breath forced from her lungs. Mindy's scalp prickled. She gulped hot, stagnant air. Her eyelids fluttered open to a mosaic of green leaves.

"I liked my old chronolyzer better," Jasper said. "A bastard, but less bossy."

Your old model was too permissive.

"Since you're so keen on keeping things on track," Jasper said, "could I trouble you to dial us up some period clothes for our clothing receivers?"

Mindy felt the fabric melt onto her body. She looked down at her clothes. "No, no, no. No way am I wearing this. We're in the middle of the woods. I won't be able to make it twenty feet in this getup."

Mindy ruffled her hoop skirt. Plaid wool fabric billowed out around her, reinforced by some kind of stiff support. Every part of her body felt either weighted down or cinched in. Her shoes were too tight, and her corset made it difficult to turn, much less bend at the waist. And of course there were no comfy pockets like in her favorite hoodie.

Jasper laughed, his eyes twinkling. "You look ready for a hike to me. If it gets too hot, the chronolyzer and I can rest in the shade of your skirt."

"You wish. At least you have pants. All I've got is these." Mindy pulled up her skirt a few inches to reveal poofy pantaloons that gathered at her ankles.

"Sexy, Gold. Very sexy," Jasper said.

"Enough all ready. Where the heck are we?" The dense woods that surrounded them gave no clue as to their location. The leaves were full and green, with none on the ground. Blackberry bushes bristled in thick clumps. Not far off, Mindy thought she heard the murmur of running water, a creek or small stream.

Jasper fiddled with the chronolyzer. "The more important question is *when*. Between that beach umbrella of a gown of yours and the wool full-front frockcoat, vest, and suspenders I'm wearing, it appears we're in the mid-eighteen-hundreds."

1861, TO BE PRECISE, the chronolyzer typed.

"Hey chronolyzer, dial me up some alternate clothes, will you?" Mindy said.

NEGATIVE. WHAT YOU ARE WEARING IS COMPLETELY APPROPRIATE.

"But I'm not comfortable."

You're an agent of the Free Fascist State now, Gold. Your discomfort is in the service of human autonomy and stability.

"Well, that's comforting, but it's easy for you to blather on about service to the state. You're just a stupid machine. You don't have to wear twenty pounds of ugly wool plaid in heat like this."

I see you have no interest in approaching this situation rationally, the chronolyzer typed. I've nothing further to say to you until you calm down. The chronolyzer screen went black.

Jasper rolled his eyes at the machine. "Don't even talk to it, Mindy. You'll only annoy it."

"I annoyed it? I can't believe that patronizing—"

The excited murmur of male voices bubbled through the woods.

"Get down," Jasper said. "Someone's coming."

From the chronolyzer's hard drive . . .

Civil War Countdown:

10 Figures Who Helped Split the Nation (or Pull It Back Together Again)

#10: John Wilkes Booth (1838–1865)

A successful stage actor from a long line of successful stage actors, Maryland-born Booth decided his legacy would be better served in another line of work. An ardent supporter of the Confederacy and slavery, Booth's most famous role was as assassin. Early in the day on April 14, 1865, Booth visited Ford's Theatre and tampered with the door of the presidential box so that it could be jammed shut from the inside. He returned that night during the third act of the comedy *Our American Cousin,* crept into the box where President Abraham Lincoln was watching the play, jammed the door, and shot the president in the back of the head, fatally wounding him. Booth jumped to the stage, where he may have broken his leg, yelled something rebellious, then embarked on a flight that took him to Virginia, where he was shot and killed by Union soldiers.

#9: Stephen A. Douglas (1813-1861)

An Illinois congressman, senator, and Democratic presidential candidate, Douglas was a statesman par excellence who led efforts to find a compromise between pro-slavery and antislavery states. (He was also, briefly, an admirer of Mary Todd, the future Mrs. Lincoln.) Though he supported slaveholding, Douglas argued in the famous Lincoln-Douglas debates of 1858 that residents of a state or territory should be free to ban slavery if that was the will of the people. Pro-slavery Southern Democrats weren't convinced: After all, if some states abolished slavery, pretty soon everybody might abolish slavery. In the campaign of 1860, the Democrats abandoned Douglas, their party's presidential contender, and put up a candidate of their own: John C. Breckenridge of Kentucky. With Democratic voters split, the Republican candidate, one Abraham Lincoln, snuck into office.

#8: Pierre Gustave Toutant de Beauregard (1818-1893)

As General of the Confederacy, Louisiana native P. G. T. Beauregard commanded troops in major battles ranging all the way from the bombardment of Fort Sumter, South Carolina, at the very beginning of the war, to the defense of Richmond at war's end. Beauregard's victory at the First Battle of Bull Run (also known as First Manassas), which ended in the panicked retreat of the Union soldiers, shocked many Northerners who had assumed that the war would be short and that the South would be easy to subdue. This victory, only twenty miles from the capitol in D.C., showed the Union that the Confederate Army was no joke. After the war, Beauregard received offers from both Egypt and Romania to command their national armies, but he turned them down, opting instead for a career as a businessman and city official in New Orleans.

#7: James Buchanan (1791–1868)

The only unmarried president, Buchanan presided over the country when the first seven Southern states seceded from the Union. Although he protested that secession was illegal, he also believed that he had no power to prevent secession, and that going to war against the rebel states would be just as illegal. So he did what any responsible president would do: absolutely nothing. Buchanan's inaction had the unfortunate effect of slowing the Union's preparation for conflict. For his inactions leading to war, among other crises that his administration sustained, Buchanan has been called the worst president of the United States by many historians.

#6: Jefferson Davis (1808–1889)

Although his lasting legacy comes from his role as president of the Confederate States of America, before the war Davis had been a hero of the Mexican-American War, a U.S. senator, and U.S. secretary of state under President Franklin Pierce. As CSA president, Jefferson lacked Lincoln's toughness, resolve, and diplomatic abilities. Of course, the Union's overwhelming advantage in resources and manpower didn't make governing any easier for him.

#5: William Tecumseh Sherman (1820–1891)

Cump, as friends called him, was Major General of the U.S. Army, commanding general of the Military Division of the Mississippi, and perhaps the most hated man in the South, even today. Sherman's famous March to the Sea in 1865, a devastating invasion leaving a trail of near-complete destruction, is considered an early example of modern warfare. The general believed in "total war," a self-explanatory phrase, which breaks the enemy's body and spirit. In short, Sherman's army burned, stole, or smashed to pieces virtually every community, plantation, and farmstead between Atlanta and Savannah. It destroyed crops, blew up railroads and bridges, and slaughtered livestock. Credited with the saying "war is hell," Sherman also said, upon hearing of the South's succession, "You people of the South don't know what you're doing . . . war is a terrible thing." It would appear so.

#4: Robert E. Lee (1807–1870)

Veteran commander of the Confederacy's army, Lee was arguably the South's most effective weapon. In a strange twist of fate, Lee, a career U.S. Army officer, was initially offered command of the Union forces in 1861. Loyal to his secessionist home of Virginia, he refused the honor. In June and July of 1862, Lee's Army of Northern Virginia kept the Union's Army of the Potomac from invading Richmond, saving the Confederacy from an early exit from the war. Among his other victories, the Battle of Chancellorsville in 1863 is particularly impressive because Lee's force was outnumbered by more than two to one. Although his successes in Virginia frustrated President Lincoln and Union commanders, Lee failed at both of his attempts to invade the North.

#3: Ulysses S. Grant (1822–1885)

In his early years, Grant was a failed businessman and farmer. Later, he became the resilient and creative commander of the U.S. Army and creator of the strategy that eventually wore down Confederate general Robert E. Lee's armies. He rode that wave all the way to the White House in 1868, where he served two scandal-fraught terms as president. Later in life, Grant entered into a financial venture that ultimately failed and left him desperate. So, as many a cash-strapped former leader of the free world has done, he decided to pen his memoirs, hoping to leave money for his family after he died. The scheme worked.

#2: Harriet Beecher Stowe (1811–1896)

Novelist, essayist, lecturer, and philanthropist, Stowe wrote the 1852 bestseller *Uncle Tom's Cabin: Or Life Among the Lowly,* which galvanized abolitionist sentiment in the northern United States while antagonizing the defenders of slavery in the South. A story about runaway slaves and brutal white masters, *Uncle Tom's Cabin* was the most widely read and hotly debated novel of the nineteenth century. Like other contemporaries of Stowe's, Abraham Lincoln cited the book as a cause of the war, going so far as to say, upon meeting Stowe, "So this is the little lady who made this big war."

#1: Abraham Lincoln (1809–1865)

You saw this one coming, didn't you? The 1860 election of Lincoln was a bit of a fluke, coming about more because of a dispute among the rival Democrats than because of the power of the Republicans (or that hip beard, which didn't grow in until after the election). Between the election and Lincoln's inauguration, seven Southern states seceded from the Union. The relatively inexperienced Lincoln, determined to keep the country united, rose to the occasion. He proved a masterful wartime leader and an apt military strategist. With the one-two punch of the Emancipation Proclamation in 1863 and his Gettysburg Address later that same year, Lincoln inspired Northern unity and resolve. It was also Lincoln who, after reelection in 1864, began to plan a postwar policy of reconciliation rather than punishment of the South.

Chapter Three

Mindy froze. Get down? Was he crazy? If she got down on the ground she'd never get back up. And if she tried to hide behind a tree, it would need to be a mature redwood if it was going to have a chance of concealing her hoop skirt.

Jasper crouched behind some blackberry bushes, but all Mindy could do was hold her breath and keep her eyes peeled as the oppressive heat soaked her skin with sweat.

The voices drew nearer—the boisterous ribbing of young men.

"These socks are so scratchy I think I'd be better off replacing them with poison ivy leaves!" one man said.

"Man alive, don't take 'em off! We'd all collapse."

The men guffawed as their voices receded.

"We must be near a road," Mindy said, heading toward the area where the voices had come from. The skirt became easier to maneuver in with each step. The forest thinned, ending in a grassy shoulder and a dusty red dirt road. Jasper followed, and as they peered out from the undergrowth, a two-wheeled horse-drawn carriage drove into view. A gentleman in a stiff suit much like Jasper's held the reins as two women in lace-trimmed velvet gowns far finer than Mindy's scrunched in beside him. An oversized wicker basket hung off the back of the carriage.

"What a great adventure!" one woman said.

"I hope we don't arrive too late to see it all," the other said.

"Do you think it's some sort of Fourth of July celebration?" Mindy asked. "Fireworks or something? I mean, it looks like there's a picnic basket."

She turned around to look at Jasper, but he had disappeared.

Mindy looked about, astonished. Had something happened to him, or had he run off somewhere? And why would he do that without telling her, leaving her stranded here? She suddenly felt how dependent she was on him, and she didn't like it one bit. In the years since her father had left, she'd gotten used to looking out for herself and her sister without anyone to help.

Never mind, she thought. *I'll just go after those people and find out for myself where they're going.* She hiked up her heavy skirts and started to wade through the bushes back to the path.

"Shite! Mindy, get down!" hissed Jasper from the bushes about fifteen feet from where they had originally been hiding.

"And just where have you been, anyway?" Mindy asked, crouching down again. She felt like she'd been caught doing something stupid, and her face flushed.

"I was just having a little chat with the chronolyzer, is all. I'm expected to give regular reports."

"To *that* thing?"

Jasper shrugged. "There's a lot of protocol to observe is all," he muttered evasively, without looking up from the screen.

Mindy decided there was nothing to do but shake off her irritation—for the sake of the teen they were here to rescue, for her sister, and for Jonathan. "So is this where Andros landed with Minister Hartthorne?"

"It would appear so."

"You said Andros would body hop as soon as he got here, so Jonathan should be around here somewhere, naked and probably totally freaked out."

"Andros would need to find another body before he could hop into it. Right now we're in the middle of the woods."

"But people are passing by on that road. We should follow it, and maybe we'll find Jonathan."

The chronolyzer whirred back on. ANDROS AND THE MISSING TEEN ARE OUR PRIORITY TARGETS. LOCATION OF THE PURITAN MINISTER IS SECONDARY AND CAN ONLY BE PURSUED AFTER THE FIRST OBJECTIVE HAS BEEN MET.

"But we can't abandon Jonathan!"

YOU WILL FOLLOW THE DIRECTIVES OF THE MISSION OR YOU WILL BE SENT BACK TO YOUR OWN TIME.

Jasper touched Mindy lightly on the arm. "C'mere, Mindy. If we search for Andros, odds are pretty good that we'll find Minister Hartthorne along the way." He rubbed the back of his neck. "Time-stream investigation isn't the easiest in normal circumstances. We need the assistance of the bastard chronolyzer if we're to have any hope of finding your missing friend before Andros does."

"But we don't even know who we're after."

THE TWENTY-FIRST-CENTURY SUBJECT IS CHAD PEMBROOKE. THE ALIEN TARGET HE'S BEEN BOUND WITH IS UNKNOWN.

"Chad Pembrooke? Are you sure?" It figured. When Mindy had been blasted back to colonial Salem by a chronobomb, Chad must have been blasted to this time and place—he and his girlfriend Veronica had been standing right there when the bomb went off. Just when Chad had been starting to like her again—or at least talk to her—she had to get him sucked into a mess like this. How was she going to explain all this alien time-traveling weirdness to the coolest guy in school?

Mindy took a deep breath. *Why should I be nervous around Chad?* she thought. *I'm the one who kept us from getting strung up as witches in Salem. I can do this.*

Jasper ran his delicate little fingers through his curly brown hair, pulling it back hard. "What difference does it make which person it is? A twenty-first century teen, no matter who it is, should be pretty easy to spot a century and a half in the past."

"What, because we're all the same? All twenty-first-century teens are interchangeable? If that's the case, why even bother coming back for all of them?"

Jasper leaned forward. "Sure and I'm only trying to look on the bright side, Mindy. I don't want to be here any more than you."

Mindy looked down and fussed with one of the wrist buttons on her long, full sleeves. "I'm sorry, Jasper. I—"

"Stow the melodrama and let's get moving. We need to go where the people are to determine the best way to proceed."

Mindy threw her hands up. "Didn't I just say that?"

Jasper shook his head in exasperation and started down the road.

Keeping her skirt lifted a few inches, Mindy picked her way along the narrow road as she struggled to keep up with the little man.

"If it's a picnic," Mindy said, "it should be pretty easy to spot Chad in his host body. Chad's a militant vegetarian. If he's got any control of the host body at all, he'll be throwing a fit." Mindy smirked as she thought of Chad's cafeteria sit-in protesting Salem High School's ground-organ-meats-three-times-a-week policy. He thought it weakened his skateboarding performance. Mindy wasn't keen on the hot dogs, bologna, and mystery meat that the cafeteria served, however, because she knew where meat came from. She loved animals and couldn't imagine eating one of her friends.

Behind them, a delivery wagon covered by a grayish-white tarp rattled along the road, its wheels thudding over the ruts. The time travelers stepped onto the grassy shoulder to let the wagon by, but instead of passing, the man in the front seat reined back the horses and stopped.

"Afternoon, miss," the man said, tipping his straw hat at her, "and sir. May I inquire where you're a'headed?"

Jasper spoke. "Up the road a wee bit."

"Do you think that's wise, walking through here with a lady?" the wagon driver asked. He wore a cream linen duster coat that was already smudged with the orange dust of the road. He had curly brown hair, wire-rimmed glasses, and beneath a scraggly beard, a kind, sincere look about him.

Mindy fanned herself with her hand, batting her eyelashes like Scarlet O'Hara in *Gone with the Wind*. "Goodness, I do hope it's not too much farther."

Facing away from the driver, Jasper rolled his eyes at her.

The wagon driver wiped his forehead with a grubby, yellowed handkerchief, then blew his nose into it before extending his hand down to Jasper.

"My name's O'Sullivan, Ned O'Sullivan."

The time-cop reached his delicate hand up and shook the man's calloused, dirt-smeared one with a smile. "I'm Jasper Gordon, and this is my good friend Mindy Gold. Sure and our wagon broke down a little ways back."

Mindy nodded at her introduction, wondering if she should curtsy or something.

"Well, folks," said the wagon driver, "I just wouldn't feel right leaving you in such dire straights, you being from the old country and all—and with a lady to protect too. I'm supposed to be meeting my boss, but I can take you down the road a spell."

Mindy struggled with the urge to tell the kind yet chauvinistic stranger that she was more than capable of taking care of herself, thank you very much, but her feet already hurt in the low-healed, leather lace-up ankle boots she wore. What she wouldn't give for a good pair of Keds. "We'd be delighted!" she said.

"Miss Gold can ride up front with me, but you'll have to ride standing up in the door well in the back. I'm afraid there's not much room in the photography wagon. It's a top rail darkroom, and it's not meant to carry passengers."

Mindy followed the bearded man to the back of his wagon. Jars of chemicals nestled in crates. Three empty sinks surrounded the small square of space where Mindy assumed the photographer usually stood to develop his photographs.

"Watch out for the chemicals. Might get a bit noisy too. The metal and glass clatter something fierce when the horses get moving."

Jasper wrinkled his nose. "Sure and it smells like ammonia back here," he said uneasily. Mindy, being a bit of a bio-chem geek at school, didn't mind the fumes.

Ned O'Sullivan helped Mindy into the front seat of the wagon. When he shook the reins, the horses plodded forward. The progress was slow, and the woods blocked out any breeze that might have benefited her. Debris littered the road—backpacks, bags of what looked like flour or maybe beans, wool coats with capes, and leather shoes that looked brand new. She even saw a gun or two—heavy revolvers that looked like they'd stepped out of some pirate movie. She guessed

1861 had just as many litterbugs as the twenty-first century.

Once in a while she'd hear other groups of people talking off in the woods. She wondered whether Jonathan might be among the picnic-goers. He might not have clothes, but he was very smart and would figure out a way to get some. He'd find a way to blend in, she was sure.

Unless Andros was still riding around inside of him. The Galagian had said he enjoyed making the minister misbehave, and a naked, possessed minister could get into a lot of trouble with very little prodding.

But Jasper had said Andros would leap as soon as he got a chance. That meant he could be inside anyone—anyone at all.

Ned cocked his head and grinned at her, wiping the sweat from his brow.

Mindy swallowed hard. Her scalp tingled. Was that an alien grin? Alien sweat? She wasn't good at starting conversations herself, but she had to try. She had to figure out if Ned was possessed by Andros. "So, have you been taking photographs long?" she squeaked.

"A while."

"Seems like a lot of equipment to be hauling around."

"I don't, usually. The field wagon is brand new, made special for the occasion. My boss has a studio back in Washington—the biggest on Broadway. All the prominent men and women of Washington want to sit for us. Even President and Mrs. Lincoln have been to our studio."

"How exciting," Mindy said.

"Yeah, my boss loves his studio. Me, though, I like it out here." He waved his arms expansively. "I think it's much more interesting to be out of doors."

As Ned continued chatting, Mindy let herself relax. He seemed like a kind and genuine man. If Andros was inside of him, he was doing a good job hiding it.

Despite the toll the jolting of the wagon was taking on her butt, Mindy enjoyed the ride. Ned had a team of two beautiful bay quarter horses. She loved watching their muscles ripple beneath their red-dish-brown coats and their black manes ruffle as they trotted along, towing the wagon with ease. The smell of two sweaty horses might bother some people, but it reminded her of the time her dad took her horseback riding. Since her dad moved to Florida after her parents' divorce, she hadn't seen much of him. The last time he'd flown her down for a visit, he'd taken her horseback riding. That was almost three years ago.

Ned reined the horses at the top of the rise, and the landscape opened into a field dotted with an occasional tree. A small town hud-dled before them, and between them and it lay tens of thousands of soldiers in blue and gray uniforms.

Mindy's stomach sank. This was no picnic they were going to. This was a war. There would be no potato salad and fried chicken to share with Chad. There would only be blood and bullets.

"Centreville," Ned said. "Rumor has it that tomorrow the Union marches on Manassas Junction to stomp those Confederate seces-sionists good."

The blood drained from Mindy's cheeks, and all feeling slipped away. How was she ever going to be able to find Chad and the alien amid an ocean of soldiers?

On the Home Front:

5 Ways That Civilians Got Involved in the Civil War

Civilians didn't just sit around having picnics all day while the troops were off fighting the war. Many good-natured folks took to constructive activities like beating the daylights out of their political opponents and, well, having picnics.

#1: Dole out beatings

Think politics is boring? Not during the Civil War era! During the long buildup to the war, Charles Sumner, abolitionist senator from Massachusetts, delivered an antislavery speech, going so far as to insult pro-slavery colleague Andrew B. Butler. The South Carolina congressman and his nephew Preston S. Brooks entered the U.S. Senate chamber, confronted Sumner at his desk, and beat the defenseless senator with a cane until the cane broke. Sumner was so badly injured that it was three years before he could return to work. When news reached South Carolina, dozens of Brooks's constituents sent him new canes with notes of congratulation. An approving editorial in the *Richmond Enquirer* crowed, "We consider the act good in conception, better in execution, and best of all in consequences." Congressman Brooks later apologized, sort of. He said he meant no disrespect to the U.S. Senate. This was good enough for the House, which voted not to oust Brooks for his somewhat aggressive debating tactics.

#2: Feast on sandwiches and deviled eggs

In July 1861, Union troops marched out of Washington and toward the strategic railroad junction at nearby Manassas, Virginia. The war was barely three months old, and many Northern politicos assumed that a quick victory was at hand. They figured the Federal boys would easily whip the Confederates camped at Manassas, move on to capture the Confederate capital at Richmond, and be home in time for lunch. God bless America!

On July 21, hundreds of civilians rode out in carriages to watch the brewing battle. They brought picnic baskets filled with delicacies and fine wines. An English journalist covering the battle quoted a well-dressed woman watching the action through opera glasses as saying, "That is splendid . . . Oh, my! Is not that first rate? I guess we will be in Richmond this time tomorrow."

Not quite. The woman and her companions were no doubt shocked when Confederate reinforcements arrived and the undisciplined Federals were forced into a disorganized retreat. Frightened picnickers found themselves witnessing the First Battle of Bull Run, a humiliating defeat for the North. The fine carriages hurriedly turned and joined the stream of soldiers skedaddling back to Washington.

#3: Protest and loot

By spring 1863, the Confederate capital of Richmond was in worse shape economically than many other parts of the South . . . and the rest of the South was in shambles. Much of the war had been fought nearby, ruining crops and tearing up farmland. Prices for ordinary staples such as bread were seven times higher than they had been two years earlier. On April 2, a group of several dozen women marched to Capitol Square to protest the high cost of food. Virginia governor John Letcher was unable to placate the crowd, which grew to as many as a thousand. The women rampaged through the streets, shouting "Bread! Bread!" smashing windows, and looting stores. President Jefferson Davis arrived, scrambled up on a wagon, and began throwing Confederate currency into the air and shouting, "You say you are hungry and have no money! Here is all I have!" It wasn't much, but he had caught the women's attention. Davis then said that if they didn't leave the street in five minutes, he would order the militia to open fire. They opted to take the money and run.

#4: Attack and riot

In 1863, Congress passed the nation's first-ever conscription act, introducing the country to the dreaded draft. Working-class men in New York, especially in Irish American neighborhoods, bitterly resented the draft. They believed rich men were unfairly forcing poor men to fight their war for them, which wasn't too far from the truth. And, as with everything at the time, there was a racist angle to the affair. False rumors spread that the government was bringing runaway slaves into the city to take the jobs of drafted whites. On July 13, the anger turned to violence. Mobs attacked draft offices, police stations, and the pro-war *New York Tribune* newspaper. They beat or lynched any unfortunate African American they happened to see. Several brigades of Federal troops were rushed into the city to combat the rioters, but the three days of violence claimed more than 300 civilian lives.

#5: Dodge the draft

The working classes were on to something when they suspected they were fighting for the rich. The most controversial part of the new draft law was a provision allowing a drafted man to shirk his duty legally by paying a $300 commutation fee. Of course, that meant those who could afford the fee didn't have to go to war (ah, democracy!). Among the sons of the wealthy, one twenty-six-year-old lawyer named Grover Cleveland took advantage of the nifty loophole. Instead of risking his hide on the battlefield, he paid the fee and, in 1863, became assistant district attorney of Erie County, New York. Cleveland did have a halfway decent reason to stay out of the army: He was supporting his widowed mother. Still, when Cleveland launched his political career, his avoidance of service provided ammunition to opposing campaigns. But because most Northerners were as racist as Southerners, and many others were apolitical and not really concerned about whether the states got back together, the fact that Cleveland had weaseled out of fighting wasn't too shocking. Cleveland went on to win elections for the offices of county sheriff, mayor of Buffalo, governor of New York, and, in 1884, president of the United States.

Chapter Four

"Are those Union or Confederate soldiers?" Mindy asked.

The photographer eyed her suspiciously. "Them's our boys, of course. The Union forever!"

"But the uniforms," Mindy said. "Why are they blue and gray?"

"What other colors would they be? Blue's regular army, gray's for militia volunteers. There's all kinds of uniforms, especially among the three-month volunteers. There's a whole regiment of New York firemen dressed in red pantaloons and red fezzes with blue tassels, of all things. The Fire Zouaves, they call themselves. And when the troops paraded through Washington, I even saw one division wearing kilts!"

A muffled voice called from the back of the wagon. "Right. Are we there yet?" Jasper asked.

"Yeah, but you might not like where *there* is," Mindy answered as Jasper clambered out of the wagon.

The sprightly Time Stream Investigator whistled when he saw the wide expanse filled with men. The rolling hills overflowed with men and muskets, horses and wagons—thousands of them. "Thunderin' Jaysus," he said softly.

"I don't know how we'll ever find our friend Chad," Mindy said.

"What division is he?" Ned asked.

"Umm . . ." Mindy stalled.

Jasper interrupted. "Sure and could you tell us the date?"

"What?" Ned raised a bushy eyebrow.

"The date, man. The day and the month, you know."

"Saturday, July twentieth," Ned said.

As Jasper surreptitiously punched information into the chrono-lyzer he'd slipped into his pocket, Mindy leaned over and whispered to Ned, "He's not from around here. And he's not like other people. He mixes things up sometimes."

Ned nodded sagely.

Jasper hadn't heard Mindy's exchange with Ned, or if he had, he ignored it. "I'm afraid we've got bigger problems than finding young Chad amid all these soldier fellas. According to the chronolyzer, we're looking at Brigadier General Irvin McDowell's Union camp the night before the Battle of Bull Run."

"Okay, and?"

"By this time tomorrow, of the thirty thousand Union troops down there, more than three thousand will be dead, mortally wounded, or captured."

Mindy batted her eyelashes at Ned. "Would you excuse us, please?" She took Jasper's arm and led him out of Ned's earshot.

"*Hello*—knowledge of future events—ever think that maybe I don't want to get accused of being a witch again?" Mindy growled. "I'd prefer not to hang."

"Sure and we're not in 1692 Massachusetts anymore, Mindy Gold. They don't hang you for being a witch around here."

"How about spies, then? Do they execute spies in 1861? Because that's what you're going to sound like if you keep spouting random chronolyzer trivia."

"Whisht, girl! You'll make the machine fecking mad again!"

said Jasper, looking down at the chronolyzer.

It typed Too late, and turned itself off.

"Never mind," Jasper said with a scowl. "The bastard thing's borderline broken anyway. And here's what you need to know: The Union forces move on Manassas Junction at two o'clock tomorrow morning. If we don't find young Chad in the next eight hours, there's a good chance he won't make it through the next forty-eight."

"I'm going to need sunglasses if you keep up your blinding optimism, Mr. Sunshine," Mindy said. "Give me the chronolyzer. I'll just apologize to it."

"Em. I doubt that's going to help."

"You just don't know how to talk to people."

Mindy took the chronolyzer from Jasper. She addressed the electronic device as if intoning a spell. "Oh chronolyzer of wisdom, oracle of all that's known, Yoda of the twenty-sixth century, share your knowledge with us, your unworthy carriers."

It powered on.

No, it typed, but it didn't turn off. It was a start.

"Pretty please with sugar on top?" she begged.

Pleadings based on food have no influence on me.

"Pretty please with forty-two-grillion-six-hundred-twenty-seven tetra gigs of memory on top?"

Better, but no.

"But we're too stupid to figure it out without you," Mindy said.

Which is apparent when you use the word "grillion" as if it were a real number. It paused, then typed, So what do you want to know?

"Tell me about the battle we're evidently about to witness."

At 2:00 a.m. on Sunday, July 21st, 1861, Brigadier General Irvin McDowell's 30,000 Union troops will face off against Brigadier General

G. T. Beuregard's comparably sized Confederate force at a small yet pivotal railroad depot in northern Virginia, not twenty-five miles from the nation's capitol. This first major land engagement of the Civil War will be called the Battle of Manassas by the Confederacy, which named battles after the nearest town. The Union, which named battles after the nearest body of water, will call it the Battle of Bull Run.

Fighting at Bull Run will be brief but fierce, led on both sides by inexperienced officers and even greener recruits. In under twenty-four hours, the Confederacy will have soundly trounced the Union, sending the invading army of the North back to Washington, D.C., with its tail between its collective legs.

"So how are we going to find Chad?" Mindy asked.

That part's for you and Officer Gordon to figure out.

Jasper cut in. "That *is* our job, Mindy. And I'm sure you'll make it easier. One twenty-first-century teen should be able to spot another twenty-first-century teen."

"But there are too many men here! We'll never find him in time."

That's all you're going to get from me. Telling you how to do your job might make me appear "bossy," the chronolyzer typed before turning off again.

A sarcastic edge tinged Mindy's voice. "Well, that was useful. Who knew fascist robots were so sensitive, anyway?"

Jasper sighed. "I warned you."

"There's got to be a way to find Chad, to sort through all these people. We've got to narrow the possibilities."

"Sure and if we can just cram this tiny vial of tempose into the right body, the spirit of young Chad and Andros's renegade alien friend go flying out back where they came from." Jasper handed her a glass vial of clear liquid. Mindy tucked it in her sleeve. Tempose, as

Jasper had explained to her in Salem, was the mysterious substance that made it possible for humans to time-travel. Human beings from Jasper's time tended to produce it naturally because of a genetic mutation. But tempose was also what made humans susceptible to possession by the alien race called the Galagians, who craved tempose and preyed upon humans for it. Chad had been given one dose of tempose by the chronobomb that sent him back in time, and they would have to give him another dose of it to make his spirit time travel again.

"Yeah, but we have to find the right body first—the one that has Chad and the alien inside it," Mindy said. "Hey, maybe that's it: The distinguishing characteristic of our host body is that it contains three spirits or essences—the person who actually owns the body, plus the two visitors. Is there a way we can pick up on that?"

"In 2512, the chronopolice could use sensors to detect multiple essences in one body. But we don't have anything like that in 1861."

"Would a photograph work?" Mindy asked.

Jasper rubbed the back of his neck thoughtfully. "I don't know. Maybe. Photographers are using a wet-plate photography process at this particular moment in history, so it might pick up a spirit image. But we don't have a camera."

"Ned does. Wait here." Mindy sashayed back toward Ned, enjoying the way her skirt whooshed in front of her.

"I'm going to have to be headin' on, Miss Gold," Ned said, pushing back his straw hat and wiping his forehead again. "I've got pictures to take, and my boss is waiting for me somewhere on the other side of camp."

"It's a shame, really," Mindy said.

"What's a shame?"

"That the light will be so poor by the time you get way over there." Mindy waved a hand in the general direction of the encampment.

"There should be plenty tomorrow to take an image," Ned said.

"I suppose, but we're on the eve of a history-changing moment. Don't you think there should be some record of, well, the magnitude of it all?"

"That's why I'm here, Miss Gold. I really must be moseying on."

"Of course, of course. It's just such a nice, expansive view." Mindy threw her arms open wide. "Nothing like you'd get in a studio."

Ned scratched the side of his nose. "Maybe I should set up here and expose a few."

"Do you mind if I watch?" Mindy asked, opening her eyes wide. "I find the whole process so . . . fascinating." Mindy hated sounding like some vapid cheerleader flirting with the quarterback, but she didn't have any choice.

"I expect not," Ned said.

Mindy hoped that meant yes.

Ned took a huge box from the covered wagon and set it up on a tripod, again checking the shot. From a dust-proof box, he removed an eight-by-ten glass plate.

"This is the collodion," he said, mixing chemicals from jars labeled "guncotton," "sulfuric ether," "alcohol," "bromide," and "iodide of potassium."

"You coat the plate with collodion and then wait until the ether and alcohol evaporate a bit. Gotta get the plate all nice and sticky. The rest I've gotta do underneath the cover. Gotta have it extra-dark. Nobody move until I come back out or you'll blur the shot. Shouldn't take more than a couple minutes to coat it with silver nitrate, expose it for about twenty seconds, and then develop it," he said, turning back to the camera and ducking under the dark cloth that kept light from entering the camera.

Mindy waited impatiently as Ned completed the process underneath the camera's hood. Finally he emerged with a glass plate holder. "Now I've got to go fix it and wash and varnish it back in the wagon," he said. "It'll only take a few minutes."

Mindy turned around to tell this news to Jasper, but the little man was nowhere in sight. For the second time that day, he had vanished the moment her back was turned. She cast her gaze about in annoyance, searching for him. It seemed to Mindy that on this journey she was the only one doing anything productive. She had gotten Ned to make this exposure, and whether it worked or not, she didn't see Jasper doing anything to find Chad. Apparently he couldn't even stay around to see if the photograph revealed anything.

"Where is that stupid time-cop?" she muttered under her breath. "Ned's going to want to leave before he's even looked at the picture."

"You know what your problem is, Mindy Gold?" Jasper had popped up behind her, making her jump.

"I'm stuck in the past with an unpredictable and unreliable guide?"

"Fear of abandonment."

"Just don't talk to me," she snapped, bristling. She wished she had Jonathan with them. He'd always been calm and supportive. Somehow the 300-year age difference between her and Jonathan just seemed more palatable than the 500 years she guessed separated her and Jasper.

How different things looked now that she knew Jonathan! Barely a day ago, she had been all hung up about Chad, the boy they were now seeking. After ignoring her throughout middle school, Chad had only just acknowledged her at Pioneer Village the night they were blasted back to the past. Not that she'd had much chance to enjoy it, with Veronica Stevens hanging on his arm. But now the idea of being nervous around him was a fading memory. Still, she remembered the good times they'd had as kids. He was still that little red-haired kid who assisted Dr. Mindy Gold in bandaging everything with fur or feathers in that cardboard refrigerator-carton-turned-pet-hospital.

Ned stepped out of the wagon and brought the glass plate negative over. "Here's the first one."

Mindy was stunned. Ned had captured the broad, panoramic view all right, but he'd caught something else as well. The landscape was peppered with ghostly after-images. Every soldier on the battlefield seemed to be haunted by a spectral being hovering about it. Hundreds, maybe even thousands, of Galagian aliens inhabited the bodies of Union soldiers.

From the chronolyzer's hard drive . . .

The Blue, the Gray, and the Red

5 Little-Known Facts About Civil War Uniforms

Civil War troops didn't always stick to blue or gray. Some got creative with their uniforms.

Fact #1: Some Union troops went gray

Back during the War of 1812, U.S. Army uniforms were a single shade of gray. When the Civil War rolled around, many Northern state militias, such as those from Maine, Vermont, and Wisconsin, proudly adopted "cadet gray" as their color, in defiance of any claims on the color by ol' Johnny Reb. Other Northerners wore gray after supply officers ran out of blue jackets. Other uniforms slowly changed from blue to gray as cheap cloth faded in the sun or was darned using gray fabric. Of course, all this gray occasionally led to some friendly-fire casualties.

Fact #2: Some Confederate troops went blue

The Confederates got even funkier with their colors than the North. Many Southern state militias reported for duty dressed in various shades of blue. Others wore red and green. One unit from New Orleans even decked themselves out in Revolutionary War uniforms, featuring patriot blue. To avoid falling victim to friendly fire, some blue-clad Rebs fought with their jackets turned inside out, exposing the white or tan lining.

Fact #3: Some Confederate troops wore nothing at all

At least nothing in the way of uniforms. The Confederate States of America was only two months old at the start of the war, and two months isn't a lot of time in which to equip an army. Many of the rebel volunteers arrived for duty in nothing but their work clothes. In some cases, full uniforms never arrived, and soldiers dressed piecemeal—a boot here, a jacket there. As the war wore on (pun intended), and the South's economy continued to suffer, even the meager supplies ran short. Boots gave out, but replacements weren't forthcoming. In some cases, infantry soldiers marched miles barefoot. The Confederate infantrymen who occupied Gettysburg prior to that devastating battle heard that the town had a shoe factory and came looking for it. And it soon became standard policy to swipe boots from better-shod Union counterparts who fell during battle.

Fact #4: In a pinch, butternut would do

Back in the days when people still made their own cloth, many a country boy (and most of the Southern soldiers were country boys) had a sympathetic wife or mother with a spinning wheel. With supplies running short during the war, some lucky soldiers replaced their threadbare uniforms with homespun cloth. The needle-working ladies back home could replicate the military style, but they couldn't always match the color. With good dye hard to come by, they colored their fabric in a solution made from boiled butternuts, resulting in colors that ranged from an intimidating yellow-brown to a dull orange. These corn-colored country bumpkins became known as "butternut soldiers," or just plain "butternuts."

Fact #5: Red pantaloons and fezzes were en vogue

When most people picture the typical uniform of Confederate and Union soldiers, they imagine mid-thigh-length frock coats and flat-topped kepi hats. Back in the 1860s, we still admired the French, and these uniforms were loosely based on those of the French army. But some companies took this Francophilia to the extreme, adopting the Zouave uniform of the French elite in North Africa. In the early days of the war, when men still had romantic notions of guts and glory, there was a mania for voluminous baggy pantaloons, often in bright red, and a sash at the waist that required the wearer to spin like a ballerina when putting it on. Headgear consisted of a green or yellow fez (cylindrical Turkish cap) or a white turban. Once the realities of war set in, troops abandoned the dramatic duds in favor of more practical attire.

Chapter Five

Mindy couldn't believe her eyes. Jasper had told her that Andros had brought some of his alien buddies to Earth, but she'd assumed it was a handful at most. This was not a handful.

Jasper raised an eyebrow. "Mindy, girl, are you well? You look like you saw a ghost."

Mindy felt her stomach turn over. "Thousands of them," she said weakly.

"Can't be helped," Ned said, "lessen you've got a way to tell the entire Army of the Potomac to stand still all at once."

"What?" Mindy asked.

"Even with the folks moving around makin' it a little blurry, it still looks good," he said.

"So the blurring is normal?"

"A-yup."

So these weren't Galagians—just blurry images from the lengthy exposure. Mindy recalled creating a similar effect with a digital camera on its nighttime setting.

She looked at the plate again. Not only was it blurry in spots, but it was a reverse-image negative, so everything was rather dark and difficult to make out. If the blur was part of the process, how was she ever going to figure out which one of those soldiers contained Chad? "It's very nice indeed," she said to Ned.

Jasper strode over, glanced at the negative, and said, "There. It's that one."

Mindy squinted at the figure. "It's like that all over. What's different about this spot?"

Jasper shook his head. "You notice how in all these figures, the blur stretches out in one direction—behind each man as he moves."

Mindy nodded.

"In *this* one, three separate and dissimilar blurs are radiating outward from the central image. Three spirits attached to one body. That's our guy."

Mindy tossed her head impatiently. "Are you sure?"

"Yes. That's the one."

Mindy felt the knot in her stomach loosen, but she wasn't out of the woods yet. "But how are we going to find this guy among all the others? They all look the same to me."

"He's leaning up against that tree outside that row of lean-tos along the fence. He's probably writing a letter," Jasper said. "If we hurry, we'll be able to catch up with him before he's finished."

"Now, wait a minute," said Mindy, drawing Jasper aside. "If that's Chad—or an alien—why would he be leaning up against a tree writing a letter? Wouldn't he be running around like a lunatic, tearing his hair out and wondering how he got in that body?"

"Well, he *might* do that, but more likely Chad's spirit—and the Galagian's spirit—would lie dormant for a while after entering the new body. Whoever's body they landed in would still be in control, and first he'd be unaware he was inhabited. As Chad and the Galagian woke up, they would first feel like voices inside that person's head, and then, when they were fully awake, the three would struggle for control of the body, with the strongest winning out."

"So our best chance is to get to him before Chad's really aware of where he is—before he or the alien can get into real trouble?"

Jasper nodded. "Sure and we'd better get going after our friend," he said so Ned could hear.

Ned eyed them suspiciously, but his inquiry was sincere. "You can tell that this man is your friend, from this far away?"

"Yeah," Mindy said, hoping not to push the issue any further. "We really appreciate the ride, Ned. We'll walk from here."

Ned pushed his straw hat up on his head. "Please be careful, Miss Gold. An army encampment isn't the safest place for a lady of your grace and beauty."

Jasper coughed. "I'll make certain the lady's looked after."

Mindy rolled her eyes as Ned mounted the wagon and rode off in the other direction. Soon the wagon with the beautiful bay quarter horses was out of site.

As Mindy walked beside Jasper, she felt the eyes of the soldiers on her. She hadn't seen another woman since the carriage had passed their hiding spot in the woods when they first arrived. She wondered where they'd gone to.

"Hey, darling," one of the soldiers said, dropping in to walk beside her. "What you pullin' foot for?"

Mindy's scalp prickled. Imagining she were Veronica Stevens, she summoned all the snootiness she could. "I have an appointment I must keep."

"I'd like to make one with you after you're done with this shrimp," he said, leering. It reminded her of the slick, smooth grin Andros had pulled across Jonathan's face.

The soldier's buddy joined them, walking backward in front of Mindy and Jasper, slowing their pace. "I got me about three dollars in silver," he said, tossing a bag to his friend. "That should cover horizontal refreshments for both of us."

Mindy felt the heat rise in her cheeks. The men thought she was a prostitute.

"You lot leave her alone," Jasper said, his voice deeper and stronger than she'd ever heard it before. It didn't seem to make a difference.

"Come on now, little fella, you can't keep her all to yourself. We could all use a little entertainment tonight. Hell, tomorrow we could all be dead!"

Mindy narrowed her eyes. That was it. She wasn't going to put up with treatment like this, and she certainly wasn't going to count on Jasper to defend her honor. It was up to her, and she had the skills. Her mom made her take this stupid self-defense class at the YMCA over the summer. At the time, she'd thought it the dumbest thing on the planet, especially because it cut down the number of hours she could volunteer at Dr. Plotnik's veterinary clinic. But right now she was thankful for every boring minute of it.

Think, Mindy, think, she chastised herself.

In the class, they'd taught her to find a police officer or head into the nearest store if she were being followed. So what was the 1861 equivalent of a cop or a 7-Eleven?

Mindy scanned the area and found the answer dismounting from a gallant Morgan horse not fifty feet away. She veered away from the creeps and headed for the man wearing a crimson sash with shoulders capped in gold cording.

"Excuse me, sir—"

"That's *colonel,* ma'am," the tall officer corrected. "Colonel Jamison. How can I help you?"

"Two men are following me, making, well, indecent comments."

The tall officer straightened his stance. "We do not allow ladies to be mistreated in the Army of the Potomac. Where are these men?"

Mindy turned to indicate the two slime-buckets, but they'd of course disappeared amid the thousands of other soldiers. "They're gone."

"Cowards, they are," the colonel said. "God, no doubt, will deal with them on the battlefield."

Mindy didn't feel reassured. The officer's comment only served to remind her that they had less than eight hours to find Chad in his host body and get him to safety before the battle began.

"I truly didn't mean to trouble you," Mindy said.

"I could arrange for an escort to see you to wherever it is you're headed, ma'am."

Mindy considered the offer, but as long as she wore what was evidently suggestive clothing for 1861, she'd continue to have the same problem as soon as the escort left her.

"No. No thank you, Colonel. My cousin Jasper can escort me. We're not far from our destination anyhow. Thank you so much for your help." Not waiting for a response, Mindy linked her arm in Jasper's and headed at a fast clip away from the officer and the slimy soldiers.

Once they got out of earshot, Jasper cleared his throat. "Sure and an escort might not have been a bad idea, *cousin*."

"But then I couldn't do this," she said, reaching into Jasper's pocket. She pulled out the chronolyzer and held it in the crook of her elbow, her billowy sleeve obscuring the device from prying eyes. "Chronolyzer," she whispered. "I'm really standing out, here. What other roles did women play during the early days of the Civil War? Maybe I could pose as something a bit less, well, conspicuous?"

Apparently happy to be asked its opinion again, the chronolyzer rapidly typed its response. YOU'VE BASICALLY GOT THREE OPTIONS:

1. NURSE. THOUSANDS OF WOMEN LIKE CLARA BARTON AND DORTHEA DIX TOOK CARE OF THE SICK AND WOUNDED TROOPS.

PROS: NURSES WERE WELL-RESPECTED AND NOBODY MESSED WITH THEM.

CONS: NOT A LOT OF NURSES AT FIRST BULL RUN. AND THE JOB ITSELF WAS A BIT GORY. I'M NOT SURE YOU COULD HANDLE IT. YOU SEEM A BIT SQUEAMISH.

Mindy decided to let the chronolyzer's comment slide. She needed information more than she needed to be right. Besides, it did kind of depend on what the chronolyzer meant by "gory." She didn't think she wanted to know.

2. SUTLER/CAMP FOLLOWER. CAMP FOLLOWERS WERE CIVILIANS WHO FOLLOWED THE TROOPS, OFFERING GOODS AND SERVICES FOR A PRICE. SOME WERE VENDORS, SELLING FOOD AND OTHER GOODS OF NECESSITY. SOME SOLD THEIR SERVICES.

"You mean like a hooker? That's what got me into this trouble."

SOME WERE PROSTITUTES, YES, BUT MANY MORE WERE HIRED BY SOLDIERS AS COOKS, SEAMSTRESSES, OR LAUNDRESSES.

PROS: LOTS OF FLEXIBILITY TO GO WHERE YOU NEED TO GO WITHOUT MILITARY INTERFERENCE.

CONS: YOU DON'T HAVE ANYTHING TO SELL, AND ODDS ARE PRETTY GOOD THAT YOU CAN'T COOK 19TH-CENTURY FOOD OVER A CAMPFIRE, OR SEW OR CLEAN LIKE A 19TH-CENTURY WOMAN.

"And the last one?" Mindy asked.

3. VIVANDIERE. ON BOTH SIDES OF THE CONFLICT, WOMEN ENLISTED TO FIGHT IN THE CIVIL WAR JUST LIKE THE MEN. SOME DONNED MODIFIED UNIFORMS THAT ALLOWED FOR SKIRTS AND OTHER FEMALE ASSETS. OTHER VIVANDIERES NEVER CONFESSED THEIR WOMANHOOD, PREFERRING INSTEAD TO POSE AS MEN FOR THE DURATION OF THE CONFLICT.

PROS: YOU'LL GET TO BE DOWN AND DIRTY WITH THE TROOPS, AND IF YOU DRESS UP AS A MAN, AT LEAST THE MAJORITY OF THE DROOL WILL STOP.

CONS: YOU COULD GET SHOT AND WIND UP DEAD, OR WORSE.

"What could be worse than being dead?" Mindy asked.

LET'S HOPE YOU NEVER HAVE TO FIND OUT.

"What about the women we saw in the wagon on our way here? What were they?"

BULL RUN WAS A UNIQUE BATTLE. THIS EARLY IN THE WAR, PEOPLE EXPECTED A BRIEF AND DECISIVE END TO THE WHOLE CONFLICT. CIVILIANS FROM WASHINGTON BROUGHT PICNIC LUNCHES TO WATCH THE FINE AND GLORIOUS BATTLE, USING A DISTANT HILL AS THEIR GRANDSTAND. MOST OF THESE WERE FROM THE GOVERNMENT—SENATORS, THEIR WIVES—WHOEVER COULD WEASEL A TRAVEL PASS OUT OF THE APPROPRIATE PEOPLE IN THE GOVERNMENT. BECAUSE YOU'RE NOT A SENATOR'S WIFE, THAT OPTION IS OUT.

Mindy wondered why the all-knowing, all-seeing chronolyzer had given her clothes that matched the one category she couldn't even fake her way into. Maybe it wasn't as omniscient as it liked to pretend.

"What do you think I'd fare best being?" Mindy asked, hoping to keep the chronolyzer engaged long enough to get an answer without annoying it so it turned itself back off again.

VIVANDIERE.

Jasper shook his head. "I don't think that's such a good idea."

"And why is that? Don't you think a woman can fight just as well as a man?"

"It's not women in general. In 2512, women share equal roles in the military. I just don't think *you* should fight," Jasper said.

"I liked your comment better when I thought you were disparaging an entire gender instead of just me."

"You're not exactly the most coordinated person in the world," Jasper said, "nor the luckiest. You're likely to get your arse shot full of buckshot."

"We're not here to fight," Mindy insisted. "We just have to find Chad, give him the tempose so he can travel back to my time, and then get the heck out of Dodge."

Jasper exhaled heavily. "Fine then, we'll be soldiers."

The chronolyzer typed, WHAT KIND OF UNIFORM WOULD YOU PREFER?

"Standard Union blues," Jasper said decisively.

THERE IS NO STANDARD UNION UNIFORM AT THE BEGINNING OF THE WAR OF THE REBELLION. UNION REGULARS WORE BLUE WOOL, BUT THEY WERE FEW AND FAR BETWEEN. NO MORE THAN 2,500 OF THE 30,000 UNION SOLDIERS AT BULL RUN WERE REGULAR ARMY.

"So give us the bastard militia uniform," Jasper snapped.

WHICH DIVISION? VOLUNTEERS CAME FROM COUNTIES ALL OVER THE UNION, AND EACH HAD ITS OWN VARIATION ON THE UNIFORM. THEY PREENED LIKE PEACOCKS DURING DRESS PARADES. GRAYS WERE MOST COMMON, BUT—

"Just pick whatever you think best, and let's get on with it."

They ducked behind a supply wagon and the chronolyzer did its thing. They emerged as fresh-faced Union militia men with full packs and complete equipment. For Mindy, the most startling addition was the musket topped with a sharp steel bayonet.

YOU ARE PRIVATES IN THE 4TH PENNSYLVANIA, the chronolyzer typed. YOU ENLISTED FOR THREE MONTHS, AND NOW THAT YOUR ENLISTMENT IS UP, EVERYONE ELSE IN YOUR REGIMENT VOTED TO LEAVE BEFORE THE BATTLE, BUT YOU OPTED TO STAY. THAT GIVES YOU A REASON TO BE IN CAMP WITHOUT THE REST OF YOUR REGIMENT.

If Mindy thought the gown had been difficult to manage, she now staggered with her thirty-pound pack as the itchy wool scratched her skin. She pulled at the back of her collar and discovered her long, curly brown hair was gone. "Chronolyzer, you didn't really cut my hair, did you?"

YOU SAID YOU WANTED TO LOOK LIKE A BOY, AND NOW YOU DO.

Jasper chuckled. "You know better than that, Gold. It's an illusion, just like the rest of your clothing."

"But my hair isn't my clothing."

"Sure and you make a handsome man, if that's any consolation," Jasper said.

"Gee, thanks." She picked at her short hair. Not even enough to pull back into a ponytail.

"According to my calculations, our target should be off somewhere to our left."

As they walked through the camp, Mindy realized that dressing like a guy didn't much help her act like one. She wasn't exactly a girlie-girl, but she felt seriously feminine when she compared herself to the soldiers around her. First, her gait had far too much sway to it. She tried to swagger while ignoring where she was stepping, but her leather brogans hurt with the first few steps.

Next she found herself pulling at the strap across the front of her single-breasted dark blue frock coat. It caught one of the nine brass buttons that went down the front of her coat. The uniform was definitely made for flat-chested guys, not girls with assets. She tried to slouch forward a bit to compensate, but the weight of her thirty-pound pack tended to pull her backward instead of forward.

As she and Jasper marched through camp, they passed hundreds of industrious young men engrossed with the ritual tasks that have always consumed soldiers the night before a large battle—prayer, writing letters to loved ones, cleaning their weapons, and idle distractions like playing cards and singing songs of home. If Jasper's information was correct, one out of every ten men she passed wouldn't make it off the battle field tomorrow.

She shifted her strap along her woolen uniform one more time. To a Confederate cannonball, she looked every other soldier. Her stomach twisted into a tight knot. She could be one of those "one in ten" soldiers who never saw home again.

Cross-Dress for Success

5 Women in Men's Uniforms

During the Civil War, women were barred from serving in the military. Still, hundreds of them infiltrated the fighting ranks by passing themselves off as men. In camps where nobody bathed, uniforms were baggy, and everyone slept in the same clothes they marched in, the ruse wasn't too tough to pull off.

Woman #1: Sarah Emma Edmonds, a.k.a. Franklin T. Thompson

Canadian-born Edmonds disguised herself as Frank Thompson and enlisted in the 2nd Michigan Infantry. She served as a medical aide in field hospitals and was then chosen to slip behind enemy lines in Virginia as a spy. Edmonds made several forays into Confederate territory. She disguised herself as, among other characters, an African American laborer and an Irish peddler named Bridget O'Shea. When Edmonds caught malaria, however, she needed medical treatment. Fearful she would be found out, she traveled back to Michigan and checked into a hospital under her real name. Once recovered, she set out to rejoin her unit, but on the way saw a poster listing Frank Thompson as a deserter. Her military career was over. After the war, Edmonds married and had three children. Her war memoir was a bestseller, and she was cleared of the desertion charge, which meant she could receive her veteran's pension of twelve dollars per month.

Woman #2: Amy Clarke, a.k.a. Richard Anderson

When Walter Clarke of Tishomingo County, Mississippi, enlisted in a Confederate cavalry unit, his wife, Amy, decided to join him. Disguised as a teenage boy, the thirty-year-old woman fought at the Battle of Shiloh in 1862, where her husband was killed. According to the *Jackson Mississippian* newspaper, she fought valiantly and sustained two wounds, one to the ankle and the other to the chest. It's likely her secret was discovered as a result of the wounds, and she was mustered out of the cavalry. But as soon as she was well enough, she enlisted in the 11th Tennessee Infantry, under the name Richard Anderson. Little is known about her service after that, but by some accounts she won a field promotion to lieutenant. One unconfirmed story has it that Union troops captured her, discovered her secret, and sent her back to her own side wearing a dress.

Woman #3: Sarah Rosetta Wakeman, a.k.a. Edwin Wakeman, a.k.a. Lyons Wakeman

As a young single woman, Sarah R. Wakeman realized that men's jobs paid better than women's. Disguised as Edwin Wakeman, she found work on a coal barge on the Susquehanna River in Upstate New York. While on the river, she met soldiers of the 153rd New York Regiment who were on their way south. The soldiers urged young Edwin to enlist. She agreed, and on August 30, 1862, she gave the name Lyons Wakeman to the recruiting officer. After her regiment was defeated along the Red River in 1864, Wakeman stayed behind in a New Orleans hospital, suffering from dysentery. She died of the disease the next month.

Woman #4: Jennie Irene Hodgers, a.k.a. Albert D. J. Cashier

According to one of several conflicting stories, the preteen Jennie Hodgers may have dressed as a boy to get a job in a shoe factory. According to other versions, she cross-dressed for the first time on July 2, 1862, the day she enlisted in the 95th Illinois Infantry. It is known for sure that young Jennie, a.k.a. Albert Cashier, fought in the battles of Nashville, Mobile, and Vicksburg, as well as the Red River Campaign in Louisiana. Once captured by Confederates, the five-foot-three-inch woman snatched a gun from her guard, clubbed him with it, and escaped. Unlike most of the women soldiers of the Civil War, Hodgers decided she liked the feel of men's clothes and continued to live as a man after the war. She settled in Saunemin, Illinois, where she held positions such as farm hand, janitor, and town lamplighter. In 1910, after a car hit Jennie/Albert, the doctor who treated her learned the secret but kept it quiet. A few years later, Jennie/Albert became mentally incompetent. She spent her final two years in the women's ward of an insane asylum, forced to wear a dress. Her Saunemin friends saw to it that she was buried in uniform, with the name Albert D. J. Cashier on her grave marker.

Woman #5: Loreta Janeta Velazquez, a.k.a. Harry T. Buford

Loreta Velazquez's published account of her incredible Civil War adventures is a fun read, although some of its claims may be inflated. The daughter of a Spanish government official in Cuba, Velazquez said she ran away from a New Orleans boarding school at age fourteen and married an American army officer. When the war broke out, her husband joined the Confederates. Unwilling to stay at home, she disguised herself as an officer and traveled to Arkansas to recruit men for her own infantry brigade. After traveling with her 236 men by boat down the Mississippi and across the Gulf of Mexico, she found her husband in Florida and reported for duty. He recognized her but went along with the ruse until he died in a training accident a few months later. Velazquez claimed in her memoirs to have fought at the First Battle of Bull Run before changing back into women's clothes and infiltrating Washington, D.C., society as a Confederate spy, at one point meeting President Lincoln. She also saw action in Tennessee at the siege of Fort Donelson and the Battle of Shiloh, where she was reunited with her Arkansas recruits.

Chapter Six

Mindy tried to shake the dark thought of their certain demise from her head. She wanted to bolt, to beg the chronolyzer to send her back to the safety of her boring, middle class, twenty-first-century life. But she couldn't. She had to find Chad and send him home. She wasn't going to leave her friend.

A little after six o'clock, Mindy and Jasper reached a row of cedar and pine bough lean-tos along a split-rail fence.

"Our Joe should be right around here," Jasper said. "He was writing his letter right beneath this hickory tree."

The little camp was empty.

The smell of boiling rice and beans greeted Mindy's nose. In other places, the fires smelled of bacon and corn meal. She hadn't realized how hungry she was until that moment. "This way," she said, following her nose. If she didn't find Chad, at least she'd find a meal. Just beyond the lean-tos, a small group of soldiers in gray gathered around a campfire. It wouldn't make sense to find Confederate soldiers in the middle of a Union encampment, so Mindy hoped their gray pants, loose-fitting gray shirts, and turned-up hats meant they were one of the militia units Ned had told her about.

The chronolyzer typed, ASK THEM IF YOU CAN JOIN THEIR MESS FOR THE NIGHT.

"Their mess?" Mindy whispered. "Isn't that a bit rude?"

It's their food preparation group. Most soldiers didn't have cooks. They just joined up with several of their friends in the same company to take turns cooking.

Jasper took the lead. "Sure and can we join your mess, friends?"

"What do you have to chip in?" the lieutenant stirring the kettle asked. He had wavy blond hair and a patchy goatee. Although he was probably seven years older than the others around the campfire, he looked barely twenty-five.

"Whatever's in our packs," Jasper answered truthfully, taking off his backpack. Mindy did the same, though with a little more effort. Nothing looked like food at first, but she found a small stash of crackers inside a pouch wrapped up in her blanket roll. She held them up.

"Hardtack?" the lieutenant said. "Is that supposed to be a joke?"

As she spoke, Mindy's words came out too high for a guy, then descended as she tried to turn up the bass. "No . . . sir—"

"We've all got plenty of sheet-iron crackers, as you know. What's your name, Private?"

"Min—er . . ." She couldn't tell them her real name, and she couldn't think of a single guy's name that began with *Min*. The first words out of her mouth had given her away.

"Well, Private Minner, what's your first name?"

Again, she struggled to keep her voice deep and consistent. "Well . . ."

"Will, huh? There's a guy over in the First Rhode Island named Will—William, actually."

The soldier with short-cropped red hair spoke up. "Nobody calls him that—'ceptin' maybe you and his ma." He laughed out loud as if he'd said something funny. This man struck Mindy as being the joker of the group.

"Stow it, Woodbury," the lieutenant said.

The tall, skinny redhead smirked, showing a gap where he'd lost a tooth.

Jasper stepped up. "Sure and that's what we call him in the Fourth Pennsylvania," he said, clapping Mindy on the shoulder. "Plain old Will. Good-hearted Will. *Ball*-breaking Will."

"That's who you're with—the Fourth Pennsylvania?"

"Sure and we used to be, until the cowards turned tail and ran away this afternoon."

The lieutenant's gaze clouded. "I'd heard that some of the three-month men decided to head home now that their enlistment was up."

"Aye, and we're the only ones left, but we're ready for the fight."

A quiet, slender young man with haunted, hollow eyes said, "We'll all see the elephant soon enough."

Woodbury whistled through his missing tooth. "And then it's on to Richmond!"

Two black-haired, blue-eyed soldiers who at first glance looked like twins, but turned out to be cousins, joined in the cheer, shouting, "On to Richmond!" The slender youth next to them stayed silent, as did a tall, extremely muscular soldier who sat a little off to himself looking at the campfire and paying little mind to the newcomers. Looking at the tall one, Mindy marveled at how nature could produce such an intimidating physical specimen in an age without steroids.

Mindy pulled Jasper aside. "So if Chad were in one of these men, you'd figure he'd recognize me and say something, right? Or that he'd already have taken over the body and started freaking out? Maybe he's not in this campsite."

"It's hard to tell," Jasper whispered back. "He could recognize you, or his spirit could still be dormant, or the alien could be the strongest one and take over the body. Aliens usually are the dominant ones—though not always."

"Thanks, that's helpful," Mindy said, rolling her eyes.

"Just keep your eyes peeled for any odd behavior," Jasper hissed.

"Pull up a stump and have some dinner with us then," the lieutenant said.

Mindy sat next to the small, quiet soldier, and Jasper took a spot next to the giant, brooding one. *How big was the soldier in the photograph?* Mindy wondered. It was hard to tell now. And they all looked so young. If Chad truly was inside one of these inexperienced soldiers, his odds of surviving weren't good.

Still uncomfortable masquerading as a man, Mindy ate her bean dinner and drank her coffee in silence. The bean and rice soup was tolerable, but there was no meat on the menu. Mindy had formed a sort of half-baked plan that one of the soldiers would refuse to eat meat, revealing that Chad's vegetarian spirit had started to wake up and take over. With that plan dashed she'd just have to talk to each one of them and see if she could identify some signs, if not of Chad, then of alien possession.

As they ate, Jasper moved next to Mindy and whispered in her ear, "I'm pretty sure it's that great hulking lad over there with the short fuzzy hair—Anderson is his name."

"What—you think Chad and the alien are inside him? Why?" Mindy had started to fix her sights on the slender, haunted-looking soldier, Alexander.

"Look at the big lug there, all brooding and uncommunicative, like he's about to bite through a piece of plywood. There's a lot going on under there."

"Well, talk to him or something."

"Sure and I will, as soon as I can get five minutes alone with him without that great gobshite Woodbury yakking my ear off." He turned back to the others.

After dinner, Alexander, the soldier with the haunted gaze, was assigned cleanup duty as the junior member of the mess.

"Want some help?" Mindy asked, eager for an opportunity to get to know one of the soldiers better.

"Sure," Alexander said, biting his lower lip thoughtfully.

They took the tin plates, cups, and utensils to the river and rinsed them in some of the dirtiest water Mindy had ever seen. Downriver not forty feet Mindy saw a soldier relieving himself in the water.

"Have you been with the army long?" Mindy asked, trying not to think about what might be happening upriver—or what she'd do when she had to relieve herself.

"The whole regiment mustered in the beginning of June. Lieutenant Barbara recruited most of us. He was our teacher back in the day."

"It's good to be with your friends. Must remind you of home," Mindy said, hoping to remind Chad of his twenty-first-century home, if he was in there.

"It's why we're fighting," Alexander said. "It's for our family and friends back home."

Mindy finished rinsing the last plate in the muddy water.

"We'll all find out what we're made of tomorrow, won't we?" Alexander said, handing the stacked dishes to Mindy and gathering up the kettle and other utensils.

Mindy didn't know what to say. She knew the battle was going to be an unexpectedly bloody one, and an embarrassing defeat for the

Union, followed by four long years of misery. She decided she'd better say nothing.

Alexander continued. "It's just that the only gun I've ever fired is my pa's old squirrel rifle, and that's only about twice. Not that I'm worried about freezing up or anything," he added hastily.

"I know you won't," Mindy said. "Everyone has more inside of them than they think they do."

Back at the campfire, Anderson and the black-haired cousins Parker and Elisha played cards as Jasper watched. They looked so much alike that Mindy couldn't tell between them enough to be able to remember which of them had won from hand to hand. It didn't help that the cards didn't have numbers on them—just the suites and figures. Mindy had no idea what they were playing, even. She knew Jasper didn't either, but the sprightly time-cop seemed to take a delight in watching the game anyhow.

The soldier named Oliver leaned with his back against a hickory tree, writing a letter like the multiple-spectral-image soldier in Ned's photograph. Mindy sat down next to him.

"Writing home?" Mindy asked. She thought it was funny how her biggest investigative technique was to ask an obvious question. It seemed to work, though, and that's all that mattered.

Oliver nodded, chewing on the end of a cedar pencil. "To Lorena."

"Your fiancée?" Mindy guessed.

"If I make it back home alive and able to provide."

"Well, dead guys don't make good husbands," Mindy joked.

Oliver frowned. "No, they don't."

Mindy felt like an idiot.

Oliver returned his focus to his letter, chewing on his cedar pencil as he agonized over the next word.

"Is she pretty?"

Oliver sighed. "Prettier than a summer sunset over Langston Pond back home."

"That's what you should write."

He brightened, then carefully penned a line.

"Do you miss her?"

"More than I miss our outhouse and my old coon dog Buster."

Mindy smiled. "Maybe you should stick with telling her how pretty she is."

Oliver nodded. Encouraged, he again contemplated his letter.

Mindy leaned back against the other side of the hickory, watching the cousins play cards. Jasper had joined in and seemed to be doing well, laughing and joking easily with the other soldiers as he shuffled and rearranged the cards in his hands. In fact, as Mindy shortly realized, the little Irishman must be doing *really* well, as they'd made him the dealer.

As Jasper passed out the cards, he nodded easily to each of the men in turn. "So where might you be from, Anderson?" He inquired with an amiable look.

The big man's voice was deep and gruff. "Philadelphia," he stated simply.

"Ah, is that so?" said Jasper in his lilting, lyrical accent. "A city boy. I would have never guessed. With great big muscles like that, I'd have pegged you as a farmer for sure."

Anderson said nothing, but his brow darkened.

"And your voice, now, Anderson. It has the melodious lilt of the Appalachians. Or maybe 'tis the sound of the majestic Mississippi River I'm hearing. I'm from the old country—I can hear these things, you know. And you don't sound like a Yankee to me."

"I tell you I'm from Philadelphia," barked Anderson angrily, looking intently at his cards.

"Ah, now don't take offense. I was only thinking of how wonderful it is that the music of this great country's local dialects isn't restricted to one place but spread out all over and mixed about, so that even in Philadelphia you can hear a bit of the Appalachians."

Anderson said nothing, studying his cards stony-faced.

"From Philadelphia, then. And what part, may I ask?"

Anderson looked up and stared Jasper in the face, the whites of his eyes glinting in the firelight. "Market Street. Just east of the Delaware River."

"Just east of the Delaware River, you say?"

"That's right." Anderson glowered defiantly.

"You did say east, did you not?"

Anderson threw down his cards and stood up, facing Jasper. "I said east, dammit. Why? What business is it of yours?" His great hands bunched into fists. Across the campsite, people had stopped talking to listen to them.

Jasper smiled and spoke softly. "Well, it's just that east of the Delaware River you'd be in New Jersey, is all."

No one spoke. All eyes stayed glued to the two men.

"You're not from Philadelphia at all, are you, lad?" Jasper's voice was calm and measured.

The lieutenant with the goatee looked at Anderson with keen interest now. Woodbury looked back and forth between Jasper and Anderson, unsure what to do. Once again it was Jasper who broke the silence.

"Friends, I think we have an impostor in our midst. A spy."

Before anyone could move, Anderson had lunged at Jasper and

had thrown the smaller man to the ground. Before Jasper had time to react, Anderson had his boot on Jasper's throat.

"I'm a slave." Anderson's words were spoken quietly, but no one had any trouble hearing him. His voice was controlled but had a dangerous edge to it. "Is that what you wanted to hear? I'm an escaped slave." He glared around the campfire with a look of defiance. "I'm the son of a plantation owner outside Jackson, Mississippi." He stopped for a moment but did not take his foot off Jasper's throat. Still no one spoke, and after a moment he continued. "Each and every day of my life I was beaten by the other field hands because I looked whiter than the overseers. And then I was beaten by the overseers for the same reason. By the time I turned thirteen I could beat any of them, and the other slaves were too scared to touch me. But still I slept outdoors because they wouldn't allow me in the slave quarters.

"When I was seventeen, I married a woman belonging to Anderson. We had a baby, and the baby was white like me. My wife was beaten to death by the other slaves, and old man Anderson sold the baby. Then Mississippi seceded from the Union. I heard a rumor about the forming of the Army of the Potomac and I ran away from the fields to join it. Anderson's men caught me and dragged me back. They flogged me until I couldn't stand. I ran away again. They caught me again. This time I'd been caught impersonating a white man to buy passage on a riverboat. They shackled my feet and left me outside as a warning to others. They put up a sign next to me that said, 'Any man or woman who aids this escaped slave is subject to prosecution by the state of Mississippi.'

"I sat there for three days without food or water. Once a white woman came along and spoke to me. I asked her for help. She said she was from the North—an abolitionist. She said my treatment was disgraceful. I asked for water, but she read the sign and hurried away. Two days later I finally broke the shackles with my bare hands. Now I'll gladly do the same for your neck, you little Irish bastard."

"Now, lad, there's no need to get so violent. I was just twistin' your hay a little, is all."

"Back off, Anderson," the lieutenant spoke up at last. Anderson did not move.

"I'll kill any man who tries to stop me fighting in the Army of the Potomac. I've come this far. I'd rather die right here than go back."

"Settle down, Anderson," the lieutenant said. "I didn't hear any of this. I don't want to know any of this. Go to bed, both of you."

Grudgingly, the big man took his boot off Jasper, who coughed and rubbed his throat. Anderson shot Jasper a menacing look and then went to his bedroll and lay down.

From the chronolyzer's hard drive . . .

Civil War Superlatives:

The Abolitionist Yearbook

In the mighty struggle against slavery, hundreds of writers and lecturers took up pen and paper to build a case against the wretched institution.

Best Qualified: Frederick Douglass

Born Frederick Augustus Washington Bailey, the young Douglass was taught to read and write, in defiance to Maryland state law, by the wife of his owner. In 1838, at about the age of twenty, Douglass escaped his owner, fled north, and changed his last name to mask his identity. Four years later, at an abolitionist convention in Massachusetts, the young, impressive-looking African American stood up to speak about his experiences. In doing so, he provided the Massachusetts Anti-Slavery Society, sponsor of the convention, with exactly what it needed: a brilliant speaker who could talk to white audiences about what it meant to be a slave. Douglass became a popular lecturer, and his popularity grew even further with a bestselling autobiography in 1845.

Most Inspiring: Sojourner Truth

Isabella Baumfree, better known as Sojourner Truth, spent the first twenty-nine years of her life as a slave. She was sold from master to master in the villages around Kingston, New York, endured beatings, and was even forced into marriage for the purposes of breeding more slaves. She finally escaped in 1826, just a year before the state finally outlawed slavery. While working as a maid in New York City, the devoutly Christian Isabella began to preach on street corners. After a visit by the Holy Spirit called her to service, she changed her name to Sojourner Truth (no account survives to explain why). She took up a career as a traveling evangelist, spreading a religious message that embraced abolition and women's rights. Although not as polished as Douglass, the imposing six-foot-tall Truth was nonetheless a charismatic and persuasive speaker who drew large crowds in the Northeast and Midwest to hear her speak of the injustice of slavery. Once the war began, Truth recruited free blacks to fight for the Union and collected supplies for their regiments.

Most Violent: John Brown

Words weren't enough for John Brown, and his actions weren't quite as civil as those of Truth and Douglass. The Connecticut-born abolitionist and borderline crackpot believed that armed rebellion was the only way to get the job done. Although white, the industrious Brown settled his family in 1849 in an otherwise all-black community in North Elba, New York. There he and five of his grown sons (Brown fathered twenty children in all) resolved to take up arms against pro-slavery forces. In 1855, they rode to the territory of Kansas, which was bitterly divided over whether to permit slavery. After pro-slavery advocates sacked the abolitionist town of Lawrence, the Browns struck back, attacking a pro-slavery town where they dragged five men into the streets and brutally hacked them to death. Brown evaded the law, and in 1859, he and twenty-one followers invaded the small town of Harper's Ferry, Virginia, took sixty local men hostage, and took over the federal arsenal. Brown thought the dramatic crime would inspire slaves to join his "army of emancipation." After a two-day siege, U.S. Marines, under the command of U.S. Army colonel Robert E. Lee, attacked the arsenal and took Brown prisoner. Tried for treason, among other crimes, Brown was sentenced to hang. But his motives transcended his brutal and savage actions, and he became a kind of martyr.

Most Famous: Henry Ward Beecher

The closest thing to a rock star among the abolitionists, blue-eyed Beecher was a Congregational clergyman, pastor of the well-attended Plymouth Church in Brooklyn, top draw on the lecture circuit, and little brother to abolitionist author Harriett Beecher Stowe. Women in particular admired his muscular physique and energetic speaking style. Mark Twain once described Beecher in the pulpit as "discharging rockets of poetry and exploding mines of eloquence." The showman-orator used broad gestures and attention-grabbing gimmicks, such as stomping on a slave chain while he was speaking. The preacher had a little edge to him as well: His "Beecher Bibles," Sharpe rifles hidden inside Bible crates, were a popular item among abolitionists in Kansas.

Most Radical: William Lloyd Garrison

Garrison was a controversial figure, and not just because he advocated the burning of the Constitution. The Massachusetts journalist and cofounder of the American Anti-Slavery Society was a hardliner who denounced what he called "gradualists"—people who wanted to end slavery in stages or compensate slaveholders for their property. Garrison demanded total and immediate emancipation. In 1831, in the first issue of his abolitionist Boston newspaper, *The Liberator,* he wrote, "I do not wish to think, or speak, or write, with moderation . . . I am in earnest—I will not equivocate—I will not excuse—I will not retreat a single inch—AND I WILL BE HEARD!" *The Liberator* attacked the Constitution for what Garrison saw as its support of slavery, calling it "a covenant with death." His extreme views even caused a rift with fellow abolitionist and one-time admirer Frederick Douglass, who felt the Constitution could be used to fight slavery. In 1844, using the slogan "No union with slaveholders," he argued that the free states were sanctioning slavery by remaining in a union with the slaveholding states and that the North must secede. Not always consistent, Garrison later supported Lincoln's policy of fighting to preserve the Union.

Most Contrary: Lysander Spooner

Spooner fell on the other side of the Constitutional divide from Garrison. A legal scholar, philosopher, and influential pamphleteer, Spooner constructed complex arguments explaining why the Constitution was an antislavery document. But Lysander wasn't all fun and games: Touting his philosophy of "individual anarchy," he not only called for an end to slavery, but he also advocated slaves using violence to win their own freedom. Yet Spooner also argued that the secessionist states were within their rights, as defined by the Constitution, to decide for themselves whether to remain part of the Union. The antislavery Spooner criticized the antislavery Republican Party for what he called its hypocrisy, condemning the party's plan to stop the spread of slavery in the new states and territories of the West while failing to confront slavery in the South. When the Lincoln administration resolved to go to war, Spooner again attacked the Republicans, arguing that the federal government was fighting for an illegal cause (the preservation of the Union) instead of a legal cause (the abolition of slavery).

Chapter Seven

Mindy helped Jasper to his feet. "Good work, genius," she said.

"How was I to know the great bloody shite would knock me to the ground?"

"Well, what did you think would happen? You can't just back people into corners, you know. Besides—"

Mindy was cut off by the arrival of a man bearing a large piece of meat. "From the quartermaster," was his only explanation. He handed it to Woodbury, then turned and walked on.

Woodbury elbowed Alexander. "Looks like you still have some mess duty," he said, handing the meat to the boy.

Alexander pushed the meat back at Woodbury. "I'm not cooking that. It's gross."

"There's not that much of it, but it'll be a good amount for each of us," Woodbury said.

"I won't cook it," Alexander said, standing taller but looking just as green.

"Why in blazes not?" Woodbury demanded.

"I don't eat meat," Alexander said.

Elisha chortled. "Since when?"

Alexander looked a bit confused himself. "Just leave me alone!" he said and stormed off across the field.

"Ungrateful shirker," Woodbury said.

Elisha clapped Woodbury on the back. "Take it easy on him. He's just worried about tomorrow." Elisha's voice lowered. "He's not even eighteen yet. He told me once that when he went to enlist he put a slip of paper in his shoe that read '18' so that when they asked him his age he could honestly say he was 'over eighteen.'"

Woodbury shrugged, trying to make light of it all. "Oh, let him go boil his shirt, for all I care. It means more for us!"

When the group turned its attention back to the cow leg, Mindy grabbed Jasper by the elbow and whispered, "Chad's inside Alexander."

"How can you be sure?" Jasper asked.

"Hello—vegetarian, remember? Chad is a vegetarian. It's happening just like I thought it would—Chad's spirit is waking up inside Alexander, and even though he doesn't recognize me yet, the first thing he's manifesting is an aversion to meat."

Jasper nodded. "Right. That's moronic, Mindy. Why would young Chad manifest himself purely in vegetarianism and not in any other way? Did it occur to you that that meat they're eating might be disgusting and maggot-ridden, dripping with blood and pus and mucus and all things foul? This *is* the Civil War, in case you'd forgotten. Highly unsanitary. Personally, I'm planning to go boil myself when all of this is over."

Mindy looked at him fiercely. "Forget you. I just know I'm right. His vegetarianism is manifesting itself before anything else either because, (a) his aversion to meat is visceral and unthinking, and therefore stronger than anything requiring his conscious mind, or (b) his vegetarianism is such a deeply held moral conviction that it manifests itself even in a semiconscious state."

"I'm still not sure any of that makes a lick of sense, but even if you *might* be right, now he's run off to God-knows-where before we can even get the chance to test your great theory."

"Well, that is a bit of a problem, but he'll be back. He's not going to wander too far on the night before a battle, right?"

Mindy thought Alexander would be back in a few minutes, but after she had waited a while, then lay down on her scratchy wool blanket on the lumpy ground to wait some more, the vegetarian private still hadn't returned.

From her bedroll, Mindy stared up at the stars. Not a cloud in the sky. The night was starting to cool, a welcome respite from the day's unrelenting heat. The chirping of katydids and the stray barking of dogs in the distance would have made the scene a languid lullaby, but tonight it was just the calm before the storm. Mindy drifted off to sleep.

A tentative whisper woke her.

"Minner?"

"Uh huh . . . " Mindy answered without opening her eyes.

"It's Alexander."

Mindy was suddenly wide awake. She didn't know how much of Alexander was Chad and how much was Alexander—or Andros's alien friend for that matter—so she decided to stay in character as much as possible. "We're glad you're back."

"I'm not a coward. I just needed time to think," he said. "Things seem to be getting all mixed up in my head—that's all."

Mindy nodded. "It's going to be a big day tomorrow. Maybe you should get some sleep." She wanted to talk to him—to Chad—but Chad didn't seem to be in control. At least not yet. And Alexander didn't seem to recognize the other spirits inside of him. If she started talking to Alexander like he was from the twenty-first century, he'd think she was crazy and avoid her, and then she wouldn't be able to keep him safe in the upcoming battle. The thought of an actual friend of hers being torn apart by bullets made her tremble.

"I guess." Alexander rolled out his blanket next to Mindy's. The last time Mindy had lay this close to Chad Pembrooke it had been in a sheet fort in her living room when they were both in fifth grade. She tried to lay still and breathe evenly as if she were asleep, but it wasn't any use. There would be no more sleep tonight. She was so certain that Chad was in there, and she needed to *do* something to help him.

"Minner?" Alexander whispered.

"Yeah?"

"If I die on the battlefield tomorrow, will you bury me?"

"You're not going to die, Alexander."

"But if I do," he insisted, "will you bury me? I want a good Christian burial, for my folks' sake."

"Stop being so morbid," Mindy said. He'd *better* not die. Her plans included rescuing him and getting the hell out of there, not tracking down Alexander's family and making funeral arrangements.

"Promise me," Alexander said. "If I die and you don't, promise me you'll bury me. I can't ask one of the other guys, 'cause it'll make me look like I've gone, well, soft like a woman."

Mindy bristled but didn't respond. She realized now how much she took her twenty-first-century liberties for granted. Equal rights for men and women and all people, regardless of their race or gender, took on a whole different meaning in 1861 Virginia.

"If it'll make you feel better, I promise I'll bury you."

"Thanks, Minner. If you die and I don't, I'll do the same for you."

Mindy's stomach sunk. She didn't want to think about that. Not at all. The ground became harder and colder, and now, no matter what she did, she knew there was no way sleep would come to her again that night.

Although she didn't sleep, Mindy dropped into a near-sleep state, almost hypnotized by the clear sky and bright stars and nearly full moon. A century and a half in the future her mom might be looking at the same stars out her little sister's hospital room window.

The earthy, nutty smell of coffee drifted through the night. Mindy rolled over and found Alexander poking the glowing orange coals of the campfire with a stick. Above it, coffee brewed. She sat up, rubbing her arms, which had grown stiff in the now-cool night.

"Coffee, huh?" Mindy said.

"Yeah."

Mindy looked closely at him for signs that he might be recognizing her as Mindy Gold from Salem High—signs that Chad was definitely in there. But still nothing.

Mindy fingered the vial of tempose Jasper had given her. There had to be a way to get herself and Chad out of this place before either had to bury the other. Sure, Jasper said that the safest way to build up a person's tempose level was to do it a little bit at a time, over two to three days, but Alex wasn't going to last two to three days, and neither was she at this rate. She had to do something, and quick.

It was time to take matters into her own hands. Who could she really depend on other than herself?

She twisted the cap to the tempose vial. "Alexander, will you hand me my canteen? It's right behind you."

When Alexander turned to dig in the dark for her canteen, Mindy upended the entire vial of tempose into Alexander's tin coffee cup.

"I don't see it, Minner," Alexander said, turning back around.

"Oh, it must be over here with my haversack," Mindy said,

while digging into her pouch.

Off in the distance, a lone drum played reveille. In a military version of Marco Polo, a drum from another unit echoed, this time a bit closer. Other campfires lit the hills as the entire camp rose for the march to battle.

Mindy watched with satisfaction as Alexander finished his coffee. They'd be out of here before sunrise. She went over to wake Jasper up. She had to poke him a couple of times before he grumpily sat up.

"I did it," Mindy whispered. "I gave Alexander the tempose."

"Right," Jasper said. "Now all we have to do is administer it several more times and then we'll be ready to extricate Chad's spirit and send him back home."

"No, that's the cool part," Mindy said. "I tripled the dosage. Chad should be ready to go home any time now." Mindy beamed. She'd probably saved all their lives.

"You *eejit!*" Jasper hissed. "You can't triple the tempose level. Sure and you probably just killed him!"

From the chronolyzer's hard drive . . .

Grub:

7 Staple Foodstuffs for Soldiers

There's an old saying that an army travels on its stomach. Unfortunately for Civil War soldiers, drive-through windows and 7-Elevens were hard to find on nineteenth-century battlefields. When it came to the army diet, dry, hard, and salty was the order of the day.

Staple #1: Coffee

Serving Suggestion: *straight-up black*

This wasn't your typical half-caf iced soy mocha latte. In fact, nothing says *army coffee* like a bitter mouthful of grounds. Soldiers in need of a caffeine fix boiled their own unfiltered campfire coffee, right in the cup. And when ground coffee was in scant supply, troops were left to roast their beans over the campfire—a great tutorial for future coffeehouse baristas, but not too fun for soldiers on the front lines. Coffee drinkers in the South were even worse off: With their ports under Union blockade, supplies of imported goods such as coffee ran out early in the war. They were forced to wing it with substitutes made of ground chicory, charred grain, and acorns. Caffeine cravings even crossed battle lines—Confederate and Union units sometimes traded tobacco for coffee under a flag of truce.

Staple #2: Hardtack

Serving Suggestions: *soaked in coffee, soaked in bacon fat, toasted, gnawed dry*

With nicknames like *tooth-duller, sheet-iron,* and *worm castle,* hardtack was a not-so-delectable mainstay of the Northern soldier's diet. Made of flour, water, and a little bit of yeast, the three-inch square crackers (also called *ship's biscuits* or *pilot bread*) were baked into a solid, bricklike consistency and often infested with insect larva. Not quite the fluffy Wonderbread we're used to. A military favorite for its low cost and durability over long periods of time, hardtack was either dipped in coffee to soften the texture and drown out the bugs, fried in bacon fat to make a dish called *skillygallee,* or just vigorously gnawed.

Staple #3: Cornmeal

Serving Suggestions: *corn mush, jonnycakes, hoecakes*

Unfortunately for the Confederacy, flour shortages in the South made hardtack hard to come by. Instead, soldiers were often treated to a ration of cornmeal, which could be mixed with water and cooked into a gritslike mush, salted or sweetened with molasses. If the cook could find a precious fresh egg or a bit of milk to hold the dough together, the mush could also be flattened into crude johnnycakes or hoecakes (so named for the hoes they were cooked on) and fried or baked.

Staple #4: Salt pork

Serving Suggestions: *salt-pork hardtack sandwich, salt-pork-on-a-stick, fried, gnawed dry*

Like your salt with a little meat on it? Salt pork was to fresh meat what hardtack was to fresh bread, except a whole lot saltier. When there was nothing better available, soldiers of both armies fell back on this salt-cured, smoke-preserved protein source—or fattier variations such as bacon or the appetizingly named "fatback," which was common among Southern troops. Salt pork for military use was usually cured to the point that it was hard and dry: It could be gnawed plain or sandwiched between a couple of hardtack biscuits. When they could, however, soldiers liked to soften up the salt pork by soaking it in water and then frying it or roasting a piece on the end of a stick.

Staple #5: "Salt horse"

Serving Suggestion: *don't!*

While a beef between the Union and Confederacy caused the outbreak of war, literal bad beef caused some gnarly illnesses among soldiers on both sides. Civil War–era salt horse wasn't really horse meat—at least it wasn't supposed to be. It was the nickname soldiers gave to salt-preserved beef, which was notoriously, and predictably, awful. It was either far too salty or flat-out rotten. Some salt horse shipments came to the troops covered with mold or even infested with maggots. Soldiers reported having to soak the meat overnight in a running stream to make it even remotely palatable.

Staple #6: Beans or peas

Serving Suggestions: *soup, porridge, plain ol' boiled*

They weren't canned or frozen or fresh in the pod. And, like so much else in the military diet, the beans and peas that Civil War soldiers carried in their haversacks (i.e., backpacks) were dry and hard. Often made into a soup or thick porridge flavored with salt pork, beans had to be soaked in water for hours, preferably overnight, before they could be cooked. You can still buy dried beans and peas in the supermarket, and many cooks swear by them as the best basis for a homemade soup.

Staple #7: Whatever you could find, buy, trade for, or steal

Serving Suggestions: *anyway, anyhow, anywhere*

Eggs, a stray chicken, ripe persimmons right off the tree, a pumpkin . . . Civil War soldiers, like soldiers throughout history, foraged for anything edible during their travels. Whether picking ripe wild blackberries or shooting and butchering a farmer's pig, soldiers got meals any way they could. Because so many items were in short supply during the war, especially in the South, a soldier could wheel and deal with townspeople to get his hands on something good—for instance, by trading three sewing needles to a country storekeeper in exchange for an exotic delicacy, such as a can of sardines. Many an honest soldier paid or traded for what he took, but those less ethically inclined simply stole what they could.

Chapter Eight

"Have you never heard of an overdose, girl?" Jasper continued, struggling to keep his voice low.

"But you told me it's a chemical that naturally occurs in the human body," Mindy said. "What harm could boosting the levels up a bit do?"

"Well, since in the history of time travel no one has ever been stupid enough to overdose a subject, we're about to find out, aren't we?"

Mindy crossed her arms over her chest. How was she supposed to know all the ins and outs of a chemical that wouldn't even be discovered for several hundred years? Mindy turned so she could watch Alexander. "He seems the same. Can't we just try to transport him?"

"Not until we know what the effects of the increased tempose levels will be," he said, turning on the chronolyzer and shading the glowing screen beneath his uniform jacket. "The chronolyzer says that there's a good chance that transporting him with the elevated tempose level would make the transport unstable."

"Meaning?"

"Meaning his spirit could detach, and instead of going home, it could go into some other body where we'd have to track it down again, or worse yet, it could get sent to the Void. Of course, he could just drop dead any second."

"So what do we do now?"

"We watch him, and when enough tempose has worn off to stabilize him, we'll transport him. That could be days, weeks, or even months."

"Jasper, Alexander isn't going to last that long. You heard what they said about him. He's the youngest, and he told me he's never even fired the rifle they issued him. There has to be a way to get the extra tempose out of him."

"We're not exactly in well-charted territory, since no one's ever been daft enough to triple-dose a subject."

"Okay, so I was stupid. Happy now? That doesn't change our problem. We need to either keep Alexander out of harm's way until we can transport him, or we need to get rid of the extra tempose sooner. I opt for option two because I don't relish having to keep myself safe in the middle of a freakin' battle, much less someone else."

"There just isn't any documented antidote for an overdose."

"That's it!" Mindy said. "We need to create an antidote."

"Are you daft? I just told you there isn't one."

The lieutenant's sharp "Fall in!" broke their conversation. Mindy asked the chronolyzer to display the properties and chemical composition of tempose, so she could at least be thinking about them, and then hurriedly packed her gear. She'd always been a bit of a biochem geek. Knowing how things worked in the body was one of the reasons she liked working at Dr. Plotnik's vet clinic. If there was an antidote to be discovered, she'd figure it out.

The regiment lined up in columns four wide, bayonets gleaming in the moonlight. Mindy took a spot beside Alexander so she could keep an eye on him. Jasper slid in on the other side.

Mindy had no idea how to handle her gun, so commands like "Shoulder arms!" and "About face!" meant nothing to her. Her responses were sluggish at best, but luckily she wasn't the only soldier to respond a bit slowly, and eventually she got the knack of it.

The column of soldiers moved haltingly at first, with as much stop and go as a Manhattan lunch-hour traffic jam. Soon it was more stop than go. Toward the front of the column, soldiers traded rifles for shovels, axes, and picks that they used to clear the path.

"What's with all the stuff in the road?" Mindy finally asked as they stood delayed for the gazillionth time in the long, arduous march.

"Presents from the graybacks," Woodbury said.

"Abatis," Parker said, as if she should know what that was.

Evidently her expression gave her ignorance away.

"When the yellow Confederates turned tail, they put obstacles in our way. They felled trees and did whatever else they could to make our lives difficult."

As the night sky lightened and the sun crept over the hills, Mindy used the last cover of darkness to plead with Alexander. In a soft and reassuring voice she said, "You know, we don't have to do this."

"Do what?"

"Fight. We could leave, right now. Nobody would notice."

"I would notice. I couldn't do that to my friends here and my family back home. I'm no coward."

"But what good are you to them if you're dead?"

"If you want to leave, Minner, go right ahead. Your three months is up. Nobody would fault you. Me, I'm ready to finally see some action. I want to see the elephant."

Mindy eyed Alexander. "That's not what you said last night."

Alexander shrugged. "You can't have any fun if all you ever do is safe stuff. That's dredger."

Mindy shuddered. That wasn't Alexander talking, and not Chad, either. The alien hitchhiker was waking up too.

After marching for almost six hours through a difficult, terminally obstructed path in the woods, Mindy and the rest of the 2nd Rhode Island Infantry found themselves in a cornfield.

"Not far to Sudley Ford now," Elisha said.

As they tromped through fields and past farmhouses, Mindy wondered about the farmers. Were they waiting to ambush them, to defend their lands, or had they fled to safety? The angry eyes of the Southerners seemed to bore into the back of her head as she passed by each dwelling.

As they climbed a small hill toward a high-roofed stone church whose only affectation was an arched doorway, Mindy wondered again about Minister Hartthorne. She hoped he'd be able to find a place to weather the battle safely.

The woods closed around the road again, and Mindy and the men around her were ordered by the lieutenant to take the skirmish line. Again, clueless, Mindy followed what Alexander and the others did. They formed a straight line that extended into the woods, each soldiers maybe five feet from the person next to him. The going was slow, and the soldiers around Mindy seemed tired, but they were still rather cheerful.

Then, off in the distance, the pop of a handful of shots sunk through the woods. The joking and good spirits stopped, and the soldiers moved forward in silence. Up ahead the woods thinned. A split-rail fence bordered the road in front of a farmhouse. The woods continued along the right.

Suddenly the whir of bullets buzzed the air above Mindy's head. All around her, soldiers threw themselves to the ground. Mindy followed. The tall sprigs of weeds obscured her view, but she could hear the volley of musket fire coming from both sides of the road, and pinning them down.

Mindy hadn't fired her rifle, but Alexander had, and his eyes sparkled with excitement as he struggled to reload his gun as he lay on the ground. The air hung with the warm and clinging smell of gunpowder.

"Reload, reload!" Alexander muttered. He sounded more like he had just run out of ammo while playing a first-person shooting game instead of while being shot at with Confederate bullets the size of quarters.

Stunned, Mindy watched as Alexander fumbled with a paper-wrapped cartridge from his cartridge box. He ripped off the top with his teeth and poured the powder down the muzzle of his gun and squeezed the minie ball in afterward. Then he slid a long rod from the side of the musket, rammed it into the barrel, and returned it to its slot. Pulling a metal cap out of a different leather pouch, he put it on a small nubbin near the trigger. He did all this while lying down. Then he aimed very carefully and pulled the trigger. The single shot blasted through the air, but the smoke from the gunpowder kept Mindy from seeing whether it made its mark.

A general on horseback picking his way along the skirmish line boomed vaguely encouraging things, but no one moved until a colonel barked specific directions.

"By the left flank—march!"

Alexander leaped to his feet, threw off his haversack and blanket, and let out the most blood-curdling scream Mindy had ever heard as he led the charge across the split-rail fence where the snipers were holed up. Mindy reluctantly followed, hoping her dinner would stay in her stomach instead of plastering the ground.

Jasper kept up beside her, but other than Alexander in front of her, only Oliver, the lovesick letter writer, remained with them. And his bravery only lasted a brief moment. A large cannon firing from atop a hill belched cannonballs the size of softballs. One shattered a fence rail as Oliver climbed over, sending shards of wood in all directions as he flailed backward, his face covered with blood.

A bullet took down the unit's flag bearer, and Alexander rushed forward to take the flag to keep it from hitting the ground.

The world around Mindy was a hissing, writhing curtain of bullets, but she had yet to see any of the Confederate soldiers.

That was about to change.

A cluster of gray-coated soldiers emerged from the side of the farmhouse and fanned out to form a line. In the very middle of the group stood a tall, muscular soldier with a weird grin on his face.

With horror, Mindy watched as Minister Hartthorne raised his musket directly at her.

More Civil War Superlatives:

The General Yearbook

Some were secretive, others were grouchy, still others were fashionistas; the generals of the Civil War weren't so different from your average high school graduating class.

Best Dressed: Winfield Scott Hancock, Union

Hancock was quite the strategist—"superb," according to Union Army commander George C. McClellan. Hancock rose to command an entire wing of the Union force at Gettysburg after the senior general fell. He was admired for his cheerful disposition, commanding voice, and liberal use of battlefield obscenities. But above all, Hancock was a perfectionist when it came to his dress. His collar and cuffs were always white when everyone else's were dingy. His pressed jacket contrasted with the dishevelment around him. Legend has it that even in the heat of battle, Hancock would pause to change into a clean shirt.

Worst Dressed: William. E. Jones, Confederacy

Confederate brigadier general William "Grumble" Jones was anything but meticulous. Photos show him in a wrinkled uniform, but in truth he often dressed in jeans, a blue striped work shirt, and a homespun jacket. General J. E. B. Stuart had the cantankerous "Grumble" court-marshaled for his insubordination, not to mention his poor fashion choices. But with good officers in short supply, General Robert E. Lee just transferred Jones to another command, where he was free to fight the war dressed as he pleased.

Most Stylish: Ambrose Everett Burnside, Union

General Burnside might not have been the best of military leaders, but he created one of the longest-lasting fashion statements. He was known for his clean-shaven chin beneath a magnificent set of whiskers that ran along his cheeks and jaw line. The look became popular among the ranks, with many officers sporting what came to be known as *burnsides*. Eventually, the syllables switched places, and the look Burnside pioneered is now called *sideburns*.

Most Unfortunate Name: Joseph Hooker, Union

Long before the Civil War, prostitutes were known as hookers. The term "Hooker's Brigade" came to refer to the women of dubious repute who followed Joseph Hooker's Union Army of the Potomac. Of course, these women were in no greater or lesser supply around Hooker's army than any other. But being stationed near D.C., in the view of civilian critics who could make the clever connection with his name, well, what could the old man expect?

Best Nickname: Old Fuss and Feathers, Union

Winfield Scott was almost eighty years old when he was named Union general-in-chief at the beginning of the war. He had been a career officer since Thomas Jefferson's presidential administration and a hero of the War of 1812 and the Mexican-American War. A fastidious disciplinarian, and prideful to boot, Scott had long been called "Old Fuss and Feathers" behind his back. (Note that Winfield Scott is not the same person as Winfield Scott Hancock, whose nickname was "Hancock the Superb.")Like many strict officers, and parents of teenagers, Scott was both respected and resented by his underlings—respected for his long and distinguished service and resented for what some considered his old-fashioned ideas about Army dress and deportment.

Fattest: Winfield Scott, Union

Old Fuss and Feathers wins this superlative too. It wasn't just his advanced age that kept General Scott from commanding troops in the Civil War; he was also terribly obese and suffered from gout, a painful joint condition that often occurs in the big toe. A dashing cavalryman in his youth, Scott could no longer ride a horse far enough to personally review the maneuvers of his top subordinate, George C. McClellan. This was a problem, because Scott generally disagreed with everything McClellan did. Scott had devised a strategy for victory (which was very similar to the one General Ulysses Grant would later employ to win the war), but he couldn't count on McClellan to carry it out. In November 1861, less than a year into the war, the fat and frustrated Old Fuss and Feathers gave up and retired.

Most Eccentric: Stonewall Jackson, Confederacy

Before his death on May 10, 1863, Thomas Jonathan "Stonewall" Jackson built a reputation as the ablest and most eccentric of Confederate generals, so aggressive and unpredictable that one officer serving under him remarked that he would not be surprised if Jackson ordered an attack on the

North Pole. A deeply religious man who constantly studied military history, Jackson was one of a kind. He was convinced that one of his arms was longer than the other and constantly held it up to "equalize the circulation." Shy and taciturn in his personal life, Jackson was obsessively secretive about troop movements. One night, the commander of Jackson's supply wagons, preparing for a fast start in the morning, asked the general which way to point the mules. Jackson told him to park the wagons facing the road, saying he'd find out in the morning which way to turn them.

Chapter Nine

The scene progressed in slow motion. Alexander charged forward, defenseless as he held the regimental banner high. Minister Hartthorne, in full Confederate uniform, his face dripping with sweat, pointed his musket at Alexander and fired.

Mindy watched in shock as Alexander toppled over at the impact of the bullet. The bullet caught his left leg just below the knee, and his blood splattered across Mindy's gray woolen uniform. Alexander screamed.

Mindy ran to his side, and Jasper followed.

Alexander's leg was shattered, with pieces of bone protruding from his bloody pants leg. For the first time ever, Mindy saw Jasper pale and out of control.

"Great gobshite!" Jasper said. "Holy Joe's done it now." His unhelpful profanity frayed Mindy's nerves even more.

"Shh! I'm thinking!" Mindy tried vainly to recall her veterinarian experience. "Pressure to stop the bleeding?" she mumbled. "Maybe, but that could disturb the bone."

Jasper scratched his head. "We can't pull Chad out of him in this state."

Mindy glanced up. The Confederate forces were advancing—everyone except Minister Hartthorne. He collapsed on the ground as if he'd fainted.

"We've got to get him out of here," Mindy said. Taking off her belt, she used it to tie off Alexander's leg in a tourniquet. "Help me get him to his feet."

With one arm around Mindy and the other around Jasper, Alexander weakly hopped on his good leg between them. He seemed near to fainting.

"We've got to find a doctor," Mindy said, although she hadn't seen a single physician since she'd arrived at camp, much less on the battlefield. "Ask the chronolyzer where we take him."

With his free hand, Jasper pulled the chronolyzer out of his cartridge box at his waist. "The machine says it was listening and we should have checked it before because it could have told us we were walking into a trap."

"That's not any help now. Find out where we'll find a doctor."

"The chronolyzer says the field hospital at the old stone church at Sudley Ford." He pointed to the screen, which displayed an onscreen map with a blinking green pointer.

Mindy peered at the chronolyzer's map, studying the key. "But that's . . . over a mile away! Alexander will never make it that far."

"The chronolyzer says to look for the black carriages. They're ambulance wagons."

As the Confederates marched forward on their position, Mindy scanned the battlefield for an ambulance wagon. "I can't believe Jonathan shot Alexander," Mindy said.

"Andros shot him, not Holy Joe," Jasper said, his voice losing some of its tension. "I can't believe he's still using the Rev as a host body. It's not like him."

"Andros said he liked to make good people misbehave. They don't come much better than Jonathan Hartthorne."

Jasper gagged dramatically.

"I think I see an ambulance," Mindy said. She pointed at a ten-foot wagon covered with a black tarp near the edge of the woods. Four horses pulled it along the outskirts of the battlefield. Mindy waved both arms trying to flag it down, but it headed in the other direction.

"Keep going. I'll go get them," Mindy said, running across the field to intercept the ambulance. The weeds in the field scraped at her pants legs and she had to shut her mind to the lifeless bodies she had to dodge to reach the ambulance, but she caught the wagon as it began to turn, throwing herself in front of it. "You've got to help our friend," Mindy cried.

Startled, the ambulance driver reined back the horses. "What the blazes!" He glared down at her. "Get out of my way. I've got to get these men to the field hospital."

"You've got to take my friend," Mindy said. "He's been shot in the leg."

Jasper continued to make slow progress toward the wagon with a limping Alexander leaning heavily on his shoulder. As Mindy watched, Alexander stumbled and Jasper struggled to keep him off the ground.

The ambulance driver shook his head. "I'm full up. He'll have to wait until the next run."

Mindy peered into the black covered wagon. Four stretchers of groaning, tortured men filled the back, two in the bed of the wagon and two more suspended directly above them. Three more injured men huddled on a ledge extending off the back. The box that formed the driver's seat held the ambulance driver and a younger man, probably an assistant.

"What about up there with you?" Mindy asked.

"Not with a leg injury like that. He'll never be able to climb up. He'll have to wait."

Mindy glanced back at Jasper and Alexander. Behind them, wave after wave of rebel soldiers surged across the landscape.

One of the men on the back whose bloody hand was missing three fingers groaned, "I can get up there with some help."

"Is it okay?" Mindy asked the ambulance driver.

"Just pull foot."

"Thank you, oh, thank you!" Mindy said, helping the soldier from the back into the front seat as Jasper finally arrived with Alexander and helped him onto the back ledge. The blood from Alexander's wound dripped down his pant leg, soaking his sock.

Mindy averted her gaze as the wagon pulled away.

Jasper touched her on the sleeve. "We've got to get to safety."

"We're going to follow, right? I mean we've still got to get Chad out of him before Andros gets there."

"Mindy, girl, I'm afraid we're too late. If Holy Joe saw us help Alexander into the ambulance wagon, Andros did too. There's no question he'll get to the field hospital before we will. There's nothing we can do."

"Of course there is. We just have to get to the hospital first."

Jasper shook his head. "His tempose levels will still be too high."

"So we wait until they go down, and protect him from Andros."

"You don't understand. We can't wait that long. The chronolyzer says that ninety percent of wounds like Alexander's are treated in the same manner."

"So? What's that got to do with anything?"

"Mindy, that one way, it's—" Jasper swallowed hard. "It's amputation."

Top 10:

Civil War Terms You Should Know

You've probably heard of *Uncle Tom's Cabin*. But what about Bleeding Kansas?

Term #1: Popular sovereignty

This is one of the little ideas that caused all the trouble in the first place. Popular sovereignty meant that the residents of western territories got to decide whether they wanted to be slave states. This was a fine idea as far as Southern Democrats were concerned: It kept power away from the Feds and in the hands of the states. And, of course, it was a way to keep slavery expanding westward. The Whig and Republican parties, who weren't so keen on seeing slavery spread, weren't as enthusiastic about popular sovereignty.

Term #2: Fugitive Slave Act

Part of the Compromise of 1850, the aptly named Fugitive Slave Act forced Northerners to aid in the capture of runaway slaves. As far as Southerners were concerned, this was a simple matter of property rights, but Northerners found it a little distasteful, particularly given the harsh penalties imposed on the escapees. In Boston, the unpopular act was protested by riotous crowds that had to be quelled by troops.

Term #3: Uncle Tom's Cabin

Published in 1854, this antislavery novel by Harriet Beecher Stowe convinced many readers that slavery was ultimately indefensible. It helped turn public opinion in the North even more strongly against the South.

Term #4: Kansas-Nebraska Act

The Kansas-Nebraska Act was another nifty piece of divisive legislature that helped to drive the nation further apart. Designed by that great compromiser, Senator Stephen Douglas, in 1845, this act established popular sovereignty, allowing western territories to decide whether they wanted slavery. It basically overturned the Missouri Compromise, which had prohibited slavery in those territories since 1820.

Term #5: Bleeding Kansas

No, this isn't some Civil War–era blues guitarist. Bleeding Kansas was the colorful name for the clash between the "Border Ruffians" and antislavery elements. The Border Ruffians, a group of pro-slavery Missourians, crossed over into Kansas with the intention of making it a slavery state. Perturbed by some Northern abolitionists trying to stop them, the Missourians burned down the town of Lawrence in 1856. As a counter-attack, abolitionist John Brown hacked up a bunch of the ruffians in Pottawattamie Creek, Kansas.

Term #6: Dred Scott v. Sanford

In 1857, Dred Scott came to the logical conclusion that after being taken to the free states of Illinois and Wisconsin, he was no longer a slave. He took his master to court to sue for his freedom. The case reached the Supreme Court, which came to the less than logical conclusion that Scott was not a citizen, and not even a person. Scott and every other slave were property, the court ruled, and had no rights.

Term #7: Lincoln-Douglas Debates

Back when candidate debates were still interesting events, the Senate hopefuls from Illinois, Democrat Stephen Douglas and little-known Republican Abe Lincoln, decided to go at it. Over the course of the seven debates, Douglas argued that compromises with slavery were good, while Lincoln pointed out that the compromises brought violence, that slavery was morally wrong, and that a house divided could not stand. Douglas won the debates, but Lincoln built a rep as a real nice speaker.

Term #8: Harper's Ferry Raid

Remember that John Brown guy who hacked up a bunch of people in Kansas? Seems he wasn't quite finished. After hiding out in Canada for a few years, he took his militia to Harper's Ferry, Virginia, where he captured a federal arsenal and took dozens of hostages. Brown was hoping to inspire slaves to revolt, but it didn't happen. Instead, U.S. Marines stormed the arsenal, killed a bunch of the raiders, and took the rest hostage. Convicted and hanged, Brown became a martyr for the abolitionist North.

Term #9: Emancipation Proclamation

The most pivotal document in the Civil War didn't really do very much. It wasn't until the Thirteenth Amendment passed in 1868 that slavery was truly abolished, but with the Emancipation Proclamation in 1863, Lincoln explicitly linked emancipation for all slaves to a unified Union. Although only symbolic at the time, Lincoln's act boosted morale and ennobled the North's cause.

Term #10: Hampton Roads Conference

A few months before the end of the war, bigwigs from the North and the South got together to see if they could end things peacefully. The terms from the North were simple: Agree to unconditional surrender. The Confederates were incensed, demanding complete independence instead. The two sides agreed to disagree, and the North got its unconditional surrender the hard way.

Chapter Ten

As the bile rose in the back of Mindy's throat, she realized she'd lost count of how many times the day's events had made her want to retch. "That *is* terrible," she said with a shudder. "But even if poor Alexander has his leg amputated, we can still get Chad out, right?"

"Well, we could, except over seventy-five percent of amputees die of shock or sepsis after the procedure."

"Do they *really* have to amputate?" she asked in horror.

"See for yourself," Jasper said, handing the chronolyzer to her.

"Chronolyzer, you can't be serious."

ALEXANDER WAS SHOT WITH A SPRINGFIELD .58 CALIBER RIFLED MUSKET. THIS GUN FIRES BULLETS CALLED MINIE BALLS. THEY'RE THE SIZE OF A QUARTER. WHEN THEY IMPACT A LIMB, THEY SHATTER INSIDE THE LIMB, TEARING EVERY-THING APART. EVEN YOUR EARLY-TWENTY-FIRST-CENTURY DOCTORS COULDN'T REPAIR A WOUND LIKE ALEXANDER'S WITH ANY ASSURANCE OF SUCCESS.

"But I'm sure twenty-sixth-century doctors could, right, Jasper?"

No answer.

Mindy turned and found that Jasper had disappeared.

"For God's sake!" she snapped in exasperation. This was the third—or was it fourth?—time since they'd time-traveled that he'd disappeared on her. He'd generally popped back up after a few minutes alone with the chronolyzer, but this was hardly the time or place for him to desert her.

Well, forget him. *She* had gotten Ned to take the photograph and *she* had found Chad in the campsite, and because she was still holding the stupid chronolyzer, *she* was going to rescue Chad and get them out of there. When the chips were down, you pretty much had yourself to count on and no one else.

Around Mindy, the air began to buzz with the minie balls that had made short work of the hundreds of men lying dead or dying on the battlefield.

Mindy raced for a clump of bushes along the woodline of the forest.

"Chronolyzer, there's got to be a way to create an antidote for tempose overdose."

THERE'S NEVER BEEN A NEED.

"There's no time for commentary. Show me the chemical makeup of tempose again."

The chronolyzer displayed a three-dimensional representation as well as a molecular breakdown and an analysis of its chemical properties. To most teens it would be gibberish, but not to Mindy. Bio-chem was, after all, her thing.

"Now show me a list of the chemicals found in a typical photography wagon in 1861."

LIKELY SUBSTANCES INCLUDE GUNCOTTON, SULFURIC ETHER, IODIDE OF POTASSIUM, ALCOHOL, BROMIDE—

"Wait, back up. Bromide. Is that anything like potassium bromide?"

COULD BE POTASSIUM BROMIDE OR SLIVER BROMIDE, OR MAYBE JUST THE CORE SUBSTANCE.

"Dr. Plotnik used potassium bromide in his veterinarian clinic when all those dogs got seizures. It calms animals down and dilutes the effects of the stress. Do you think it could do the same for Chad's tempose overdose?"

Possibly. It was widely used as an anticonvulsant and sedative for humans in the late nineteenth and early twentieth centuries. It's possible that we could use it to dilute the effects of the tempose, almost like siphoning the excess off. It should inhibit electrical activity in the central nervous system long enough to transport him. We'd need some of the synthetic tempose as a base, though.

Mindy rifled in her cartridge box and pulled out the small vial that had contained the tempose she doused Alexander with. "There's not much left." She held up the bottle. "Do you think it'll be enough?"

It should be. We'll mix it with water and the bromide and see what happens.

Despite the battle ranging all around her, Mindy felt for the first time that things might actually work out. She still had to find Ned and his photography wagon and manufacture the antidote, but at least she finally had a workable plan. She didn't need Jasper at all.

Ned had said he liked to take pictures of wide landscapes. *If you were going to take pictures like that of the battlefield, where would you be?* Mindy wondered.

She wished she could just hide beneath the bush until the fighting stopped, but that would be too late for Chad and Alexander. She had to get a bigger view of the battlefield and see if she could spot Ned's wagon. Summoning all the courage she had, Mindy stood up. Around her, Union soldiers started appearing, heading away from the battle. The Union forces were retreating.

Next to the bush she'd been cowering behind, an oak tree loomed. Mindy leaned her rifle against the trunk and began to climb. As she reached the top branches, bullets pattered on the leaves like raindrops. Mindy scanned the battlefield. It was hard to see any real detail because of the red dust thousands of marching soldiers stirred up, compounded with the smoke belched by thousands of firing muskets.

She couldn't really tell any specific pattern in the movement of the battle, either. Some soldiers did seem to be retreating back toward Mindy's position, but others seemed to be rushing for a small hill not far up ahead. Mindy adjusted her position to look behind her. Following the path the troops had taken through the night, she found a small white wagon parked in a clearing on an elevated piece of land. Mindy didn't recognize the wagon so much as the two beautiful bay horses with their black tails and manes. It had to be Ned.

Suddenly a harsh crack split the branch where Mindy was sitting. Splinters from an errant minie ball shot toward her, and she felt the branch jerk under her weight. The branch broke, and Mindy slid toward the ground. The branches tore at her arms and legs, scraping her face and hands as she scrambled to stop her descent. She felt as if she were back in middle school getting beat up by the class bully. Mindy fell unimpeded the last six feet to the ground, knocking the air from her lungs.

She checked briefly for broken bones and, finding none, dusted herself off and headed back down the path she'd traveled earlier, relieved to be heading away from the battlefield and toward the one thing that might get her and Chad safely home. She tried to stay to the edges of the woods so she wouldn't be spotted by snipers, but the woolen socks and her new shoes had conspired with the six-hour march last night to raise huge blisters and sores on her feet that every piece of uneven ground aggravated.

As she approached Ned's photography wagon, she wondered if

he'd recognize her as a guy. And what was she going to say to him anyhow? "Excuse me, but can I have some of your bromide so I can create an antidote for my friend who's about to have his leg amputated? See, I accidentally overdosed him on tempose, a chemical you don't even know exists, and—"

This was so stupid. She was going to be lucky if Ned didn't accidentally shoot her in all this chaos. But he couldn't shoot her if he didn't see her.

Mindy crept into the back of Ned's wagon. Using the glow of the chronolyzer's screen as a flashlight, Mindy mixed together the bromide, synthetic tempose, and water in the concentrations the chronolyzer recommended. Finding what she needed was easier than she'd thought it would be. Keeping quiet in a wagon that hung with things that rattled and clashed every time she moved, now that was tougher.

Mindy tucked the vial into her cartridge box and backed out of the photography wagon.

Behind her came a deep, melodious male voice. "Mindy Gold— what are you doing here? What is this place?"

Mindy turned to see Minister Hartthorne towering over her.

Taking a deep breath and narrowing her eyes, Mindy demanded, "What do you want, Andros?"

Minister Hartthorne looked at her quizzically. "Andros? No, Mindy, it's me. Jonathan." He took a step toward her, his large, rugged palms turned upward.

"Stay away from me. I won't kiss you again." She backed away. Andros could act like anyone he wanted when he was inside a host body, and Hartthorne had never referred to himself simply as "Jonathan" before.

Minister Hartthorne's usually clear, bright face was frantic, his brilliant emerald eyes bloodshot and frightened. "What in heaven's name is happening to me, Mindy? Since yesterday I haven't known where I am. I don't recognize anyone I see. And some . . . force has taken control of my body, making me do things I don't want to do. Surely I was wrong to doubt the existence of witches. What else can this possibly be?"

Mindy regarded him warily. Was it really the minister, or was Andros just making it sound like the minister was back in control? She decided to trust in the evidence before her eyes—the obvious terror and pain on his face. She put up her hand and touched his cheek, her eyes full of concern.

"It's not witches, Jonathan. Not exactly. But it's just as bad. Evil spirits are possessing humans, and you were possessed by a very wicked one named Andros."

"Where *are* we, Mindy?"

"We're in Virginia. I don't know how to tell you this, but . . . we're almost two hundred years in the future from your time."

"The future? How is this possible?"

"I don't really know. But you're safe now. Well, not really. But you're with me, now."

The minister's eyes widened in terror. "I shot a man, Mindy. It was horrible." His voice was hushed.

"Do you remember everything that happened while you were possessed?"

Minister Hartthorne nodded. "Do you know if he's dead?"

"I don't know. He's at the field hospital."

A second man's deep, even voice came from behind them. "Get away from my wagon, looters."

Civil War Slip-Ups:

5 Errors That Cost the South the War

Embarrassing miscalculations and bouts of carelessness weren't confined to the Confederacy. But unfortunately for the South, smaller numbers and a weaker industrial economy left less room for error. Some simple slip-ups contributed to the downfall of Johnny Reb.

Error #1: Constitutional chaos—choosing states' rights over national unity

For all the talk of states' rights, secession was essentially about slavery. But the nuts-and-bolts political argument was based on the Southern belief that the federal government had no right to infringe upon the sovereignty of individual states. Confederates thought power belonged with the states, not with a powerful central government. Of course, that sentiment carried over once they formed their own nation. State legislatures and governments— among them Georgia's, North Carolina's, and Texas's—were no more inclined to cooperate with the Confederate capital in Richmond than they were with Washington. They kept their distance by withholding troops and funds and opposing a Confederate draft. Financing a war and raising an army to fight it became a bit tricky for Jefferson Davis, especially after his vice president, Alexander Stephens, advised the states not to let the Confederate government push them around. Abraham Lincoln didn't have such problems.

Error #2: Economic egotism—assuming Confederate cotton was king

Confederate leaders saw their major export crop, cotton, as essential to textile-hungry industrial nations such as France and England. In 1860, the year before the war began, 70 percent of total U.S. exports were produced in the South, and almost all of those exports were in cotton. Many assumed that European nations would not tolerate losing their supply of this valuable commodity. In 1861, even before Southern ports came under Union blockade, cotton growers and shippers in Mississippi, Alabama, Louisiana, and Texas imposed an embargo, hoping that withholding cotton would influence Britain to intervene in the war and protect Southern ports against U.S. ships. What Southern economic strategists had failed to take into account was that British textile manufacturers, anticipating an interruption in the supply of cheap American cotton, had already built up a stockpile of the fluffy white fiber. Beyond that, there were plenty of other sources of cotton, especially for England's textile mills, because the British Empire controlled cotton-producing Egypt and India at the time.

Error #3: Diplomatic denial—thinking foreign nations would extend recognition

If the Confederacy was to achieve independence, Jefferson Davis knew, it was crucial to gain diplomatic recognition from other nations. You're not really a nation until another country—preferably, one with some clout—calls you one and sets up an embassy in your capital. Davis sent ministers to Britain, France, the Vatican, and other European nations to lobby for recognition. Davis's agents went so far as to bribe English journalists to write sympathetic stories about the Confederacy. British prime minister Henry John Temple showed some interest in recognizing the Confederacy, but he held off when Lincoln made it plain, through his own diplomatic corps, that any formal recognition of the CSA would be viewed as an act of war. After Lincoln issued his Emancipation Proclamation, Britain and the other European powers dropped any thought of recognizing the Confederacy. Lincoln had refocused the world's attention on America's Civil War as a war not just to preserve the Union but also to abolish slavery. Nobody wanted to go on record against those Union goals.

Error #4: Fatal fumble—letting a crucial military order fall into enemy hands

On September 13, 1862, Union corporal Barton W. Mitchell, stationed with his unit at a spot recently occupied by Confederate troops, found a packet of three cigars wrapped in a piece of paper. As soon as he noticed what was written on the paper, Mitchell passed the packet—cigars and all—up through the chain of command all the way to Commander General George McClellan. The paper in question: a copy of Special Order 191, issued by General Robert E. Lee three days before, detailing Lee's planned troop movements and revealing a crucial weakness: that the Confederate commander had split his forces. The information enabled McClellan's army to engage Lee at the Battle of Antietam on September 17. A horrible melee that took 22,000 lives in a single day, the battle preempted Lee's planned invasion of the North. On the strength of that Union victory, Lincoln issued his Emancipation Proclamation. Nobody knows who dropped the order that Mitchell found: It was addressed to Confederate general Daniel H. Hill, but Hill later insisted that he had never received it. The cigar-loving Hill argued that if he *had* received the packet, he would have smoked all the cigars. Maybe, or maybe it fell out of his pocket before he had a chance to light up. Either way, with that careless little accident, a Confederate invasion went up in smoke.

Error #5: Sorry surge—ordering Pickett's Charge

Called "the mistake of all mistakes" by historian Shelby Foote, Pickett's Charge was a disastrous infantry attack carried out on July 3, 1863, on the final day of the Battle of Gettysburg. General Robert E. Lee ordered the charge, sending 12,500 foot soldiers across almost a mile of open ground, directly into the cannon fire of their enemy. Lee directed the attack despite the objections of General James Longstreet, another of the commanders involved, who predicted that the plan was sure to fail. The Confederates suffered over 50 percent casualties (deaths, wounded, and troops taken prisoner). General Pickett, the movement's namesake, led his division the farthest before retreating and lost all three of its brigade commanders and thirteen of fifteen division commanders. His force shattered, Lee had to abort his second attempt at an invasion of the North. It was a major turning point, and a setback from which the Confederacy never recovered.

Chapter Eleven

Mindy heard the clatter of a trigger being cocked. "Turn around, slow-like."

She recognized Ned's voice, but she figured he wouldn't recognize her in her male disguise, and she didn't have an explanation for it. Hoping her hat obscured much of her face in the shade of the wagon, Mindy turned around, keeping her hands away from her body. Ned held a musket, pointing it somewhere between the two of them.

"Drop your weapon," Ned said.

Mindy and Hartthorne both dropped their muskets.

Ned shook his head and gestured at Mindy. "Not you, soldier. Just the enemy." He moved his aim to Jonathan.

Mindy swallowed hard. Her scalp prickled. The minister was wearing a Confederate uniform. She picked her musket back up and stepped away from him.

Hartthorne looked at her in confusion. "Mindy?"

Mindy interrupted and bellowed in her deepest guy voice, "Of course not. You're my prisoner." Following Ned's lead, she aimed her gun at Hartthorne as well.

Hartthorne held his large, rugged hands out, palms up. "Hold on there. What are you doing?"

Mindy turned to Ned. "He's battle-crazy and a little yellow, I figure.

I caught him trying to get into your wagon and stopped him. Might have been going to steal something, or maybe just hide like a cowardly Johnny Reb." She hoped fervently that Jonathan had the presence of mind to follow her lead.

Hartthorne, sharp as always, lowered his voice. "I'm frightened," he lied. "I just wanted a place to wait, until it was all over."

"I need to take him back to headquarters," Mindy said. "I'll need your wagon."

"You ain't takin' my wagon." Ned eyed Mindy suspiciously.

"I'm afraid I have to." Mindy didn't have time to spare. She had to get back to Alexander at the hospital so she could give him the antidote and they could all get out of here. Besides, what was the big deal about the wagon? Cops commandeered cars on television all the time. Weren't soldiers just like cops?

"You ain't takin' my wagon, Miss Gold," Ned said.

Well, that disguise had worked well. She wondered if all the soldiers in the 2nd Rhode Island Infantry knew she was a girl too. "I'm sorry, Ned. I've got to get out of here." She turned her musket on him.

Hartthorne raised his hands, showing his large, rough palms as he spoke. "There will be no more shooting. I will not allow another person get hurt."

"We're all going to get hurt if we don't get out of here. The Confederate forces are pushing the Union soldiers back. If we don't get back toward the hospital, we're going to be overrun by Confederates in a matter of minutes."

Ned didn't lower his musket. "You mean like him? And what are you doing in soldier clothes anyhow? You're a spy, aren't you? I heard of women sympathizers who spy for the South. You're handing off secrets to this Johnny Reb!"

Mindy's stomach turned. The situation was just getting worse. "I'm not a spy. It's just—" Mindy's voice cracked. "You were so good to me, Ned. I wish I could explain, I really do, but it's . . . complicated."

"Try."

Suddenly the woods around the little clearing came alive with the rattle of musketry. The battle lines kept receding.

"Look, how about I explain while we hightail it out of here?" Mindy pleaded.

"You're not going anywhere, spy. I'll turn you over to the real soldiers."

A minie ball went through the tarp covering the photography wagon, shattering something glass. Gray-clad soldiers emerged from the woods.

"If you think I'm a Confederate spy, turning me over to those guys is likely to get you in a bit of trouble, not us. Of course they might be Union soldiers, so if you want to take your chances, now's the time." She turned to Hartthorne. "Take the reins. We're getting out of here."

Hartthorne climbed up into the driver's seat. Mindy knew horses, but she needed to handle the gun, and a man from 1692 definitely had sufficient experience driving a horse-drawn wagon.

Ned shifted on his heels as his gaze darted between Mindy and the soldiers about a football field's length away. He looked like he wanted to shoot but wasn't sure if he should shoot the Confederates, if they were Confederates, or Mindy and Hartthorne, or both.

Mindy felt horrible. She couldn't just take his wagon and leave him to the Confederates. She already had one injury on her conscience. She couldn't take another. "We're not spies, Ned, but we do need to leave now. You can either stay here and take your chances with the soldiers and hope they're Union, or you can climb in back and come with us."

"Gol-derned thieves!" Ned said, climbing in the back of the wagon.

"Get us out of here, Jonathan," Mindy said, crawling up onto the bench seat behind the nervously whickering bay horses. He turned the wagon toward the hospital as the area swarmed with soldiers. The horses pranced skittishly away from the front lines of the battle.

"You'd better take off your jacket," Mindy said.

"That would not be appropriate in front of a lady, even one who's dressed like a man."

"Your uniform is gray."

"And so is yours."

Mindy tossed her head impatiently. "You're in Confederate gray. I'm in Union gray. We're going to a Union hospital. You don't want to be dressed like one of the bad guys."

"The Confederates are . . . an Indian tribe?" Hartthorne asked as he struggled out of his jacket.

"No, no . . . the Confederates are the Southern states of America. They wanted the states to have more authority than the federal government, and when they didn't get that, a bunch of them seceded from the Union." She was conscious that she wasn't explaining it properly.

"What does England have to say about that? We are still in the colonies, aren't we? You said this is Virginia?"

"The colonies haven't been the colonies for about eighty-five years. They became states and fought for independence from England."

The minister looked dumbfounded. He looked around in utter amazement.

"America becomes the greatest nation on the planet," Mindy

ventured. "But our Civil War is one of the bloodiest wars in history, I'm afraid. And it's only just getting started."

With the powerful bay quarter horses trotting as fast as the rut-covered road would allow them, it didn't take long to reach the field hospital at Sudley Church, a small stone church on a low hill surrounded by several farmhouses. Earlier in the day, it had been about a mile behind the main action at Bull Run. Now it was significantly closer to the fighting.

On any other beautiful Sunday afternoon, the churchyard would be filled with pious churchgoers leaving Sunday service. Instead, everywhere Mindy looked, the yard was littered with injured soldiers. The cacophony of groans and screams made Mindy's hair stand on end.

Mindy hoped she wasn't too late. Alexander had no doubt lost a lot of blood, and she didn't know exactly what might happen to Chad's spirit if Alexander died. She just couldn't let that happen. And she wouldn't.

Summoning all the courage she had, Mindy climbed down.

"Ned, we're safe," Mindy said through the canvas of the wagon. "We're at the Union field hospital. If I were you, I'd head back to Washington as quick as those two bay steeds will take you."

Ned didn't need to be told twice. He clambered up into the vacated driver's seat and urged the horses back onto the road.

Mindy didn't even know where to start looking for Alexander. He could be any of the hundreds of bodies baking in the early afternoon sun.

"We're just going to have to go from person to person. Do you remember what Alexander looks like?" Mindy asked.

Hartthorne's typically bright emerald eyes lost their spark. "I will never, ever forget that soldier's face. Or the look in his young eyes when I shot his leg out from under him."

The pain in his voice brought tears to Mindy's eyes. "Let's find him, then."

Hartthorne headed away from the church, and Mindy headed toward the stone building, milling through the mass of injured soldiers as the hot sun relentlessly beat down. Her scalp prickled. She tried not to focus on the dirt or the pain or the blood but just glanced at each man long enough to see if Alexander's haunted, hollow eyes were beneath the Hardee hat or forage cap. Mindy's eyes glazed over. So many men . . .

Without warning, a stiff hand grabbed her leg.

Timeline:

Separation Anxiety

United States? Mmmmm, not so much.

1776 1777 1791 1810 1820 1835 1836 1844 1845 1850 1852 1854 1856 1857 1860

On July 2, twelve of the thirteen colonies vote for the Lee Resolution, a document drafted by delegate Richard Henry Lee of Virginia that begins, "Resolved, That these United Colonies are, and of right ought to be, free and independent States, that they are absolved from all allegiance to the British Crown . . ." Although New York, always wanting to be different, abstains. Unanimity is not required, and the resolution passes.

On July 4, Congress approves the Declaration of Independence, a formal statement of grievances and a justification of the Lee Resolution, effectively seceding from England. Latecomer New York declares independence from Britain five days later. Goodbye Britain, hello U.S. of A.

1776 **1777** 1791 1810 1820 1835 1836 1844 1845 1850 1852 1854 1856 1857 1860

In a disputed territory claimed by both New Hampshire and New York, a feisty group of residents drafts a constitution, forms a government, and declares itself the Free and Independent Republic of Vermont on July 18.

Abandoning its claim of independent nationhood (too much paperwork), Vermont gains admission to the United States of America as the fourteenth state on March 4.

On September 28, Gulf Coast rebels declare nationhood as the Free and Independent Republic of West Florida, an area that includes parts of present-day Louisiana, Mississippi, and Alabama, but none of present-day Florida.

On October 27, the United States annexes West Florida, stating that it was part of the Louisiana Purchase, a claim that Spain had disputed. Residents, hoping to win admission to the hip new United States, are disappointed by their mother country's clinginess.

In December, President James Madison dispatches a force to take possession of West Florida. Spain says, "Go ahead, take it." Florida, welcome to the club!

On March 3, Congress passes the Missouri Compromise, a deal in which Maine joins the Union as a free state and Missouri joins as a slave state, but with the provision that slavery be prohibited in all other western territories north of Missouri's southern border. The compromise will temporarily keep the number of free states and slave states even, at twelve apiece. Are you sensing some trouble brewing?

Skirmishes develop in Texas, then in a region of northern Mexico, between local residents and Mexican troops. Rebellious Texans set up their own provisional government, formally declaring independence from Mexico a year later.

After a month of fighting during which Mexican president Santa Anna is taken prisoner, on May 14 Anna signs the Treaties of Velasco, formally recognizing the Republic of Texas.

Texas seeks U.S. statehood, but Northern resistance to the addition of another slave state stalls its efforts.

A year after pro-Texas and pro-slavery president James K. Polk takes office, Texas wins admission to the Union as the twenty-eighth state on December 29.

Protesting a recently imposed tax (isn't this why they separated from England in the first place?) on mining claims, a small town north of Sacramento, California, secedes from the Union on April 7 and declares itself the Great Republic of Rough and Ready. Less than three months later, regretful GRRR residents vote to rejoin the Union just in time for the Independence Day celebration. All of this was rather unnecessary, as the letter sent to Washington, D.C., originally declaring secession, was never acknowledged.

From September 9 to September 20, President Millard Fillmore signs into law a package of bills designed to balance the interests of free states against the interests of slave states in the Union, now greatly enlarged after the Mexican-American War (1846–1848). As part of the Compromise of 1850, California joins the Union as a free state.

1852 1854 1856 1857 1860 1861 1865 1866–1870 1939 1941 1984 1995 2005

Northern members of the Whig party, furious with fellow Whig President Fillmore for signing the Fugitive Slave Act requiring Northern states to help in the recapture of runaway slaves, block his renomination. General Winfield Scott will run on the Whig ticket and lose, effectively ending things for the Whigs and paving the way for a hot new political party, the Republicans.

1852 1854 1856 1857 1860 1861 1865 1866–1870 1939 1941 1984 1995 2005

On May 30, Congress passes the Kansas-Missouri Act, another effort at compromise between pro-slavery and antislavery factions. Sponsored by Senator Stephen A. Douglas of Illinois, it effectively repeals the Missouri Compromise by stating that residents of the territories of Kansas and Nebraska can determine for themselves whether to allow or prohibit slavery.

1852 1854 1856 1857 1860 1861 1865 1866–1870 1939 1941 1984 1995 2005

From May 21 to May 25, a pro-slavery mob, mostly from Missouri, attacks the antislavery town of Lawrence, Kansas, smashing windows, burning things, and generally making life unpleasant. In retaliation, abolitionist John Brown attacks the pro-slavery community of Pottawatomie Creek, Kansas, smashing and burning the town, and hacking up five pro-slavery activists there.

In August, President James Buchanan, concerned that Utah Territory under Governor Brigham Young will become a Mormon theocracy separate from the rest of the United States, appoints a new governor and dispatches troops to escort him to Salt Lake City.

Seeking statehood, in the fall, territorial leaders in Kansas draft the Lecompton Constitution, a proposed charter protecting the rights of slaveholders and leaving it up to voters to decide whether more slaves could be imported. The proposal spurs bitter debate in Congress, leading to a split within the Democratic Party.

In November, Abraham Lincoln, moderate Republican and former congressman from Illinois, is elected president. Lincoln owes his victory to the fractured Democratic Party, which split between Northern and Southern Democrats over the issue of slavery in the western territories.

In response to the election of Lincoln and the abolitionist sentiments of the Republican Party, South Carolina secedes from the Union on December 20.

From January 9 to January 19, Mississippi, Alabama, Georgia, and Florida secede from the Union.

On January 21, Mississippian Jefferson Davis resigns from the U.S. Senate. In his farewell speech, he calls for peace between North and South.

On January 26 and February 1, respectively, Louisiana and Texas secede from the Union.

Meeting in Montgomery, Alabama, on February 4, delegates from seven Southern states form the Confederate States of America. Jefferson Davis takes the oath of office as president five days later. So much for peace . . .

On March 2, Congress approves the Corwin Amendment to the Constitution, a desperate attempt to save the Union. If ratified, the convoluted amendment would ban any future attempt to amend the Constitution in a way that would empower the federal government to interfere with "the domestic institutions," meaning slavery, of any state. Legal scholars point out that an amendment can't ban future amendments, but the issue is moot. The Corwin Amendment is ignored by the states and never ratified.

Confederate troops commanded by General P. G. T. Beauregard open fire on Fort Sumter on April 12. The fort surrenders thirty-six hours later. Virginia, Arkansas, Tennessee, and North Carolina secede from the Union over the next few weeks. Welcome to the Civil War.

Meeting in the town of Wheeling on June 19, pro-Union Virginians opposed to secession declare the Confederate government in Richmond void and form their own state government. In 1863, they are admitted to the Union as the State of West Virginia.

1860 1861 **1865** 1865 1866-1870 1939 1941 1984 1995 2005 2006 2007 2008

Ending the last major conflict of the war, General Robert E. Lee surrenders to General Ulysses S. Grant at Appomattox Courthouse in Virginia on April 9.

The port of Galveston, Texas, the last holdout of the Confederacy, surrenders to Union forces on June 2. The war is over.

1866–1870

Over this four-year period, the former Confederate states slowly trickle back into the Union.

1939

Connecticut, Georgia, and Massachusetts finally get around to ratifying the Bill of Rights. Hey, the last century and a half was busy!

1941

On November 27, a group calling itself the State of Jefferson Citizens Committee issues a Proclamation of Independence, announcing the secession of Jefferson, an ill-defined area of northern California and southern Oregon. As of 2007, little has come of this effort.

1984

The Alaska Independence Party forms with the stated goal of an independent Alaska.

1995

At a convention in the Iolani Palace, Honolulu, on January 16, Hawaiian secession activists draft and issue a Proclamation of Restoration of the Independence of the Sovereign Nation State of Hawai'i.

2005

On October 28, a grassroots political group called the Second Vermont

Republic issues a resolution calling for Vermont to secede from the Union and "return to its natural status as an independent republic." State legislators and most Vermonters ignore them.

2006 2007 2008

On October 14, a group that maintains the 1845 annexation of Texas was illegal convenes what it calls the 11th Congress of the Constitutional Republic of Texas in Washington-on-the-Brazos, Texas.

Chapter Twelve

Mindy stifled a scream, kicking her leg to free herself. When she staggered backward far enough to see what had caught her leg, she wanted to die. She'd just kicked an injured man.

A wounded soldier with a dark stain oozing across his stomach gazed up at her deliriously. "Water . . ." he croaked.

She bent down and allowed him to drink greedily from her canteen. Others begged for her canteen as well.

"Water . . . water . . ."

Their cries made her feel like she had just walked into hell.

She had to find Alexander.

Hartthorne was walking among the dead and dying soldiers. At first he seemed like he was in a daze, but then he knelt down beside one of them, a young man with a terrible gash in his side, and took the man's hand in his own. Mindy rushed to Hartthorne's side, thinking that he'd found Alexander, but she didn't recognize the wounded man.

She started to speak to Hartthorne, thinking to pull him away to look for Alexander, but then she saw his lips moving softly as he looked into the soldier's dying eyes. He was praying.

Suddenly she remembered the chronolyzer in her cartridge box. She pulled it out. "Chronolyzer," she whispered, "where are they most likely to be keeping Alexander?"

WITH A LEG WOUND LIKE HIS, HE'S PROBABLY WAITING IN THE AMPUTATION QUEUE. LOOK FOR THE PILE OF DISCARDED ARMS AND LEGS AND YOU'RE LIKELY TO FIND HIM.

Mindy shuddered. "This is another one of your jokes, right? A pile of arms and legs? Come on . . ."

IN 1861, AMPUTATION IS THE PREFERRED METHOD OF TREATMENT FOR WOUNDS TO THE EXTREMITIES. MOST CIVIL WAR DOCTORS HAD MINIMAL EXPERIENCE WITH INTERNAL SURGERIES, PARTICULARLY THIS EARLY IN THE WAR. EVEN IF THEY HAD BEEN ABLE TO OPERATE ON BLOOD VESSELS AND DO BONE RECONSTRUCTION, THE DOCTOR-TO-PATIENT RATIO WAS ABYSMAL. AT THE START OF THE CIVIL WAR, THERE WERE MAYBE 900 DOCTORS AND OVER 300,000 SOLDIERS. EACH REGIMENT WAS ASSIGNED ONE.

"So you're saying that because they didn't have enough doctors to go around they just chopped off arms and legs willy-nilly?"

MEDICAL KNOWLEDGE WAS EVEN MORE LIMITED IN THE NINETEENTH CENTURY THAN IT IS IN YOUR TIME. NO ONE KNEW ABOUT GERMS. BECAUSE OF THE HIGH INFECTION RATE AND THE LACK OF UNDERSTANDING OF INTERNAL MEDICINE, THE LONGER THEY WAITED, THE MORE LIKELY THEY WERE TO HAVE TROUBLE. IF THEY AMPUTATED SOONER RATHER THAN LATER, THEY MIGHT SAVE THE SOLDIER'S LIFE.

Mindy couldn't believe it. She felt like she had stepped into the Dark Ages. The things these people didn't have—and, more important, the things they didn't know—made a huge difference in their world.

"We've got to find Alexander," Mindy said. She scanned the area and found the thing she'd dreaded—a pile of arms and legs.

Hartthorne showed up at her side and stared at the pile in astonishment. "What kind of barbaric place is this?"

"Let's just get this over with. We've got to make this right," Mindy said. "If we don't find Alexander and save my friend Chad, everything that's happened will be for nothing."

Hartthorne nodded. "Isaiah five-fourteen, 'Therefore hell hath enlarged itself, and hath opened his mouth, without measure,'" he said. "You are braver than any of these men—to pass through the mouth of hell for a friend."

"He was a very special friend once," Mindy said.

Hartthorne straightened himself, standing tall with his chiseled chin in the air, the fierceness returning to his piercing emerald eyes. "Let us go find your friend."

Ignoring the mound of severed limbs, they walked into the church. It had three long, bright windows on either side, but they didn't cast enough light inside. Candles and lanterns were perched haphazardly throughout—a fact that doubly disturbed Mindy when she saw that many of the injured soldiers were lying on blankets atop small mounds of hay. Some didn't even have the blankets. The entire church was a fire waiting to happen.

They scanned each face for Alexander's. Every soldier looked so young. And despite how many were here, she wondered about the hundreds, or thousands, left back on the battlefield.

Mindy tried to tell herself that each horror she passed brought her one step closer to finding Chad. It didn't help.

Then she saw it, at the back of the church. A large cluster of people that had surrounded the operating table suddenly turned and left, leaving only a surgeon, his assistant, and his lone patient.

Alexander lay on a dark and moist wooden table, a stream of blood trickling into a tub on the floor. In the tub was an arm that had been taken off at the socket. The arm's hand hung over the edge of the tub, its fingers grasping the metal as if it were still connected.

At the foot of the table stood a surgeon, his sleeves rolled up to his elbows and blood smeared across his linen apron and covering his arms. He held a sharp metal saw between his teeth. It looked more like it should be cutting through oak limbs than human limbs. The surgeon removed it and wiped it on his apron, holding it just above the wound on Alexander's leg.

This can't be happening, Mindy thought. It was like some scene out of a horror movie, a mad scientist Frankenstein taking body parts to make his monster.

Then it got worse.

The surgeon turned his head and grinned at Mindy—that same slanted grin Minister Hartthorne had worn before he shot Alexander on the battlefield.

"Mindy, how good of you to join us," Andros said, wiping sweat from his brow with the same arm that held the saw.

Borderline Cases:

4 (and a Half) Slave States That Did Not Secede

Border states were those Union states that allowed slavery but did not side with the South—at least not officially.

Border State #1: Delaware

Although slavery was legal in Delaware, the institution was not a large part of Delaware's economic or social structure when the war started, with fewer than 2,000 slaves in the whole state. In January 1861, the state legislature decided not to secede. Although dissidents from other border states formed militia companies or even regiments and joined the Confederate Army, there were no such units from Delaware. Pro-slavery sentiment ran strong enough, however, that in 1865 Delaware rejected the Thirteenth Amendment to the U.S. Constitution, which bans involuntary servitude.

Border State #2: Maryland

Maryland was a little more conflicted than Delaware. The northern half liked the North, the southern half, the South. The railroads and telegraph lines that ran throughout Maryland made it really important for troop movement and communication. Lincoln was so desperate to keep it in the Union that he offered choice military duty to keep Marylanders near their home throughout the war. Still, pro-Confederate sentiment was strong enough that, after a riot between a pro-Confederate crowd and a Massachusetts regiment left twelve civilians and four soldiers dead, President Lincoln had to declare martial law. The state government, which included many officials hostile to the Union, was dismissed, and Maryland remained under direct federal administration until the war was over.

Border State #3: Kentucky

"While I hope to have God on my side, I must have Kentucky," said President Lincoln, referring to the state's strategic importance. The Union needed Kentucky as a route for any invasion of Tennessee and other parts of the "western" Confederacy. The pro-Union legislature of this slave state voted not to secede, but early in the war Kentucky tried to stay neutral rather than fight with the Union. Governor Beriah Magoffin, a Southern sympathizer, issued a proclamation asking that no troops from either side enter the state. The Confederates disregarded the warning and stepped over into the western tip. This relatively inconsequential move sent the state legislature into a huff. Support swung to the Union. For a time, Kentucky secessionists established their own alternative state government and were even granted admission to the Confederacy. By 1863, however, there was a strong Union military presence, and the officials of the secessionist government packed up their alternate state and fled to Virginia.

Border State #4: Missouri

As with Kentucky, the Missouri legislators voted to remain with the Union while outspoken governor Claiborne F. Jackson mustered pro-Confederacy militia troops. Fearing that secessionists would overrun the U.S. arsenal at St. Louis, U.S. general Nathaniel Lyon marched on a contingent of Missouri militiamen in the spring of 1861 and took them captive. Then he force-marched his prisoners through the streets of St. Louis, an act that enflamed the ire of the citizenry. People pelted the Federals with rocks, and the troops began firing into the mob, killing more than ninety civilians. The bloody incident turned many Missourians against the Union. Jackson and his militiamen proceeded to join the Confederacy, but the deeply divided state remained under Union control throughout the war.

Secession from the Secessionists: West Virginia

Virginia's always been a bit of a oddball in the Union. Most Virginians put their loyalty to the state before their loyalty to the country. Case in point: General Robert E. Lee, who was against seccession but had to follow his state into the Confederacy. Still, when the Virginia legislature voted in favor of secession in 1861, representatives from the state's mountainous northwestern counties overwhelmingly voted against it. Outvoted by the rest of the state, the anti-secessionist Virginians decided to break away from those breaking away from the Union. They drafted an antislavery state constitution and formed a new state government based in Wheeling. Later that year, the Union army drove Confederate forces out of the region, and on the last day of 1862, the new state of West Virginia won admission to the Union.

Chapter Thirteen

Mindy couldn't believe it. After everything she had gone through, she was too late to save Chad. Andros had gotten to Alexander first.

"You're just in time," Andros continued. "I'm about to operate."

Alexander groaned.

"Ether, please," Andros said to the assistant, who evidently hadn't noticed that his superior was possessed by a Galagian.

The assistant placed a cloth over Alexander's mouth and dripped a clear liquid from a metal flask onto it. Alexander writhed and struggled as the assistant struggled alone to hold him down. Within seconds, the tension slipped from Alexander's body.

"Ether relaxes the spirit," Andros said, winking at Mindy.

Although the grisly sight had momentarily stunned Mindy, making her freeze, she now knew what she had to do.

She raced over to the table. Alexander was still awake, but he didn't seem aware of anything around him. He babbled on blissfully, making very little sense.

The assistant surgeon scowled at her. "You'll have to leave, soldier. No one but the medical staff is allowed here."

Mindy ignored him. "Alexander, can you hear me? Chad, are you in there?"

Andros sighed. "The name you're looking for is Remez. Just a few more calculations on this chronolyzer thingie and he'll be ready to come out and meet you. Or kill you. Depends on his mood."

Hartthorne swaggered forward, his piercing emerald eyes glaring at Andros. "I will not allow you to hurt anyone else." He extended his large, rough hand toward the chronolyzer. "Give me that."

Andros laughed. "You think you can intimidate me? Foolish mortal." He resumed his calculations dismissively, tapping at the screen with the handle of the bone saw as if it were a stylus. A single drop of blood dripped onto the screen.

"You will not hurt Mindy," Hartthorne said, lunging toward Andros and the chronolyzer.

Andros sliced at him with the bone saw.

Hartthorne dodged backward. He'd lost all tentativeness about him, his fiery demeanor replacing the angst he'd shown when Andros first left him.

Hartthorne slid around the amputation table. His long, muscular arms came within inches of the surgeon's wiry frame.

While Andros was distracted, Mindy slipped Alexander the antidote she had made from the chemicals in Ned's wagon. "Here, Alexander, take this."

Alexander shook his head. "I'm not thirsty. I'm just fiiine." The anesthetic had really gotten to him. Mindy eyed the bottle. The ether gave her an idea. But first she had to get Alexander to take the antidote so he could time-travel.

"Open your mouth. It's like, um, candy."

"Pop Rocks?"

Only Chad would know about Pop Rocks. Chad must be awake and aware.

"Yeah, like Pop Rocks," Mindy said.

"I don't like Pop Rocks, Mindy."

Mindy blinked, startled. "You know who I am?"

"Why shouldn't I? You've been my bestest friend forever . . . until you turned all weird in middle school . . . "

"Open your mouth, Chad."

Alexander opened his mouth, and Mindy poured the antidote down his throat.

At the foot of the table, Hartthorne barreled into the surgeon, cornering him. Andros again tried to jab at Hartthorne with the bone saw. Using his broad shoulder to pin Andros against the wall, Hartthorne grabbed his wrist and pounded it against the instrument table—once, twice, and the third time the bone saw clattered to the ground.

Triumphantly Hartthorne snatched the stolen chronolyzer from Andros's other hand. As he shoved Andros away, a heavy wooden chair came down across his back.

Hartthorne crumpled to the floor.

Behind him, Jasper stood, grinning triumphantly. "That'll teach you not to mess with a Time Stream Investigator, you great bodysnatcher!"

"Jasper, you got the wrong guy!"

"Andros was trying to grab the chronolyzer," Jasper said.

The surgeon scooped up the electronic device. "And now I have."

Jasper's grin faded. "Em. This is not good."

Mindy didn't have time to explain—only to act. She grabbed the bottle of ether and tried to douse the surgeon with it. Most of it missed, hitting the ground around him. Grabbing a nearby candle, she threw it at him, trying to ignite the flammable liquid.

The candle bounced off his chest.

"Nice try, Mindy," Andros said as he continued his calculations on the chronolyzer.

The still-burning candle rolled behind Andros, igniting the pile of ether-soaked hay behind him.

"Hey, not fair," Andros said, struggling as the flames caught his bloody apron on fire.

Suddenly the surgeon's eyes went blank and he collapsed, just like Hartthorne had done after shooting Alexander. Andros had left the body.

Cries of "Fire! Fire!" erupted in the church as the smoke started to rise.

Hartthorne groggily pushed himself off the floor, and Jasper helped him.

"Get Alexander!" Mindy cried, grabbing the stolen chronolyzer and pulling the surgeon out of the flames. She threw a blanket on top of the surgeon, extinguishing the flames.

Jasper and Hartthorne helped an ebullient and very relaxed Alexander off the table.

Chaos swarmed all around them as injured soldiers tried to get out of the burning building. Assuming Andros still had his Temporal Accelerating Device, enabling him to possess bodies whether they had tempose or not, he could be inside any one of them.

"We've got to get out of here," Mindy said.

"Wait a second," Jasper said. "Set Alexander down." He held up what looked like a clear plastic headband. "This is why I disappeared. This is what I went back to my own time to get. Each Time Stream Investigator is issued one inside his chronolyzer. Unfortunately I'd used mine back in 2512 when Andros hit me on the head, and I didn't have time to replace it." He slipped it over Alexander's injured leg.

"It's called an auto-surgeon strip." It sealed the wound closed, and in approximately fifteen seconds, whatever was inside the strip repaired Alexander's injury, even sealing back the skin without a single stitch.

"So if that's why you left, why did you stay gone so long?" Mindy asked. "I thought time travelers could, you know, travel through time."

"Well, I did come right back, as soon as I got the bastards to authorize using the bandage on Alexander, but you didn't stay put."

"I left to make an antidote for Alexander."

Jasper looked at her thoughtfully. "You like to do things your own way, don't you, Mindy girl?"

"Mindy . . ." Alexander said, still blissfully out of it from the ether.

"Well, anyway, girl, I tracked you down just as soon as I could." He took her hand awkwardly in his own. It was no bigger than her own hand.

Mindy looked into his twinkling hazel eyes. So Jasper hadn't run off on her after all.

Hartthorne cleared his throat. "There's still the little matter of this fire."

Jasper took Mindy's chronolyzer and aimed it at the burning straw. A blue-white light emitted from the end, and the fire froze into icicles that promptly began to melt.

Shaking her head in disbelief, Mindy said, "Someday you're going to have to show me how to use the advanced features of that thing."

Jasper smiled. "Ah, that's nothing."

"Mindy, I want to go home," Chad said.

Jasper scanned Alexander with the chronolyzer. "Tempose levels are within acceptable parameters. Good job, Mindy girl. Let's all go home." He pressed a button on the chronolyzer and the years swirled away, tasting of Pop Rocks and Coke.

From the chronolyzer's hard drive . . .

Sherman's March to the Sea:

How to Devastate a Countryside in 6 Easy Steps

From November 15 to December 22, 1864, Major General William Tecumseh Sherman conducted a military campaign that theorists have called the first example of modern warfare. The Savannah Campaign goes by several other names: Sherman's March to the Sea, total war, scorched earth, and several unprintable monikers coined by bitter Southerners who still hold a grudge.

Step #1: Commit to total devastation

Like his friend U. S. Grant, commander of the Union Army, Sherman believed that the only way to end a war that most Americans were thoroughly sick of was to break the South. But breaking the Southern armies strategically wasn't enough. The Confederates had shown themselves to be resilient and stubborn. The only sure way to break them was to crush them militarily, economically, and psychologically. How do you do that? Simple. You destroy every city, town, farmland, plantation, crop, livestock, and railroad line in your path. And if anyone tries to stop you, you can destroy him too.

Step #2: Steal, trample, burn, repeat

Sherman had captured the city of Atlanta two months earlier. Against the protests of the mayor and city council, he ordered the city evacuated. He kicked things off by burning Atlanta to the ground on November 15. He then issued orders for his troops to live off the land, taking what they needed as they went. This obviated the need to wait for pesky supply trains and ensured that there would be no supplies left for pesky enemy soldiers. And what Sherman's men couldn't use, they destroyed (see a theme developing here?). Sherman ordered his troops to spare the property of civilians who didn't resist, but to wreak "a devastation more or less relentless according to the measure of hostility" on those who did. The troops wreaked devastation virtually wherever they passed, on passive and hostile victims alike.

Step #3: Spread out

Sherman had 62,000 troops with him on his trek, marching in two wings that covered as wide an area as they could. At one point, Sherman had the brigades of his north flank wide of Madison, Georgia, while his south flank passed below Macon, which meant that the two wings spanned a distance of approximately sixty miles. As this condor-winged behemoth of an invasion line advanced southeast, Confederates who were attempting to mount defenses had little idea where to mass.

Step #4: Send the president a Christmas present

Confederate general William J. Hardee was hurrying his troops to protect Macon when he realized that Sherman's real objective was the strategically crucial seaport city of Savannah. Hardee got to Savannah with 10,000 troops in time to stall Sherman. After a few days of a standoff siege, however, Sherman sent his cavalry south to Fort McAllister, at the mouth of the

Ogeechee River. The horsemen captured the fort, which gave them access to the sea. A Union ship supplied them with the heavy artillery pieces they needed to complete their mission. Sherman then threatened Hardee with the big guns, demanding surrender. On December 20, the Confederates slipped away under cover of darkness, leaving the city to the Union. The next day, Sherman telegraphed the president: "I beg to present you as a Christmas gift the City of Savannah . . ."

Step #5: Tally the damage

Sherman estimated that he had destroyed $80 million worth of property of which his troops could make no use. Add to that what they took to eat, the horses and mules they used to replace their own worn-out mounts and draft animals, and any other supplies they grabbed, and, well, who's keeping track, anyway? All told, in today's currency you'd be looking at hundreds of millions of dollars, if not billions of dollars, of damage. Peeved property owners along that 300-mile-long, sixty-mile-wide swath between Atlanta and Savannah could expect no compensation. And Washington wasn't really in the business of doling out sympathy cards for wayward secessionists. The cost in lives was relatively low: only a few hundred soldiers on either side. Civilian deaths are a little trickier to calculate, especially if you factor in the people left hungry, malnourished, and vulnerable to disease in the wake of the devastation. Let's just say "total war" isn't a euphemism.

Step #6: Sit back and reflect

The March to the Sea left the South in ruins. But experts disagree about whether it was a major factor in ending the war. Sure, seeing your home destroyed before your eyes will get you down. And Sherman's tactics certainly added to a growing feeling among the Confederate troops and supporters that the cause was lost. But hungry and heartsick soldiers guarding the capital in Richmond had already started deserting by the dozens. By March 1865, General Robert E. Lee was so badly outnumbered that it was clear the end was coming. Would Lee have surrendered that April anyway, even without Sherman's tour? We'll never know.

Epilogue

From behind her surgical mask, Mindy watched as Chad, in his own body, began to wake up in his twenty-first-century hospital bed. It had taken a lot to get Jasper to let her make this visit back to her own time. She wondered how much he'd remember of their Battle of Bull Run adventure in 1861 Virginia, if anything.

Chad's voice scratched out dry and soft, but his tone was as low-key as ever. "Hey, Mindy."

"Hey, Chad."

"What's with the getup?"

"Let's just say I've developed a bit of a phobia about germs."

"You can't be any germier than you usually are."

Mindy tossed her head impatiently. "Do you know where you are, or where you've been?"

Chad sat up and rubbed his hands across his face and over the top of his head, straightening his blond hair. "Last thing I remember was walking through that lame Pioneer Village living-history place."

"Oh."

"I had some kind of funky dreams, though. I dreamed I was in this big battle, and then . . ." He swallowed hard, remembering.

"Sometimes the meds can give you weird dreams," Mindy said reassuringly. "Anyway, you'd better rest some more. I need to get back." She turned to leave.

"Mindy?"

"Yeah?"

"Why don't you like my girlfriend?"

Mindy had all kinds of answers to that one. Mostly that Veronica Stevens was an arrogant, soulless girl with a mean streak a mile long. But that's not what she said. "She's okay, I guess."

"You haven't much liked any of my friends since, like, middle school," Chad said.

"Mostly because they don't like me," Mindy said.

"They would," Chad said, "if they knew the girl I knew growing up, the girl who always cared for every animal that couldn't take care of itself, who always defended the helpless. You should let more people see that kid I knew. They'd like her."

Mindy didn't know what to say.

"I've gotta go, Chad. Get better, okay?"

"I will. And Mindy? Thanks." His chestnut brown eyes showed an intensity and a sincerity she had never seen him level on her, ever. Maybe he remembered more than she thought.

Mindy ducked into an empty bathroom and transported back to Jasper's Safe Room in 2512. She felt as though she hadn't slept in 60,000 years.

Jasper looked up from the chronolyzer. For a split second he seemed still engrossed in whatever the little electronic device was telling him, and then he beamed at her. "Gold! You're back! Skater Boy woke up safely, I assume?"

"I'm sure your chronolyzer has already told you that."

"Sure and I suppose it did," Jasper replied. He didn't stop grinning.

"What are you smiling about, Jasper?" Mindy could never tell what the little man was thinking. His unpredictability could be unsettling.

"While you were visiting young Chad, I zipped out on a little side trip. To 1865, to be exact."

"1865?" What was Jasper on about *this* time? "What on earth for?"

Jasper only smiled and handed her a very old-fashioned, sepia-toned photograph. Mindy looked at Jasper in puzzlement.

"Alexander sent you this."

Mindy looked at the photograph, puzzled. It showed a farmhouse, a cow, and a man and a woman. The man looked stiff and posed but somehow familiar. Mindy looked closer and saw that the man was indeed Alexander, but he had changed somehow. Mindy looked up at Jasper quizzically.

"It's a postcard for you from Alexander. He wanted you to have it. He also said if you were ever in Rhode Island to look him up. His farm's doing well, and he's engaged to be married."

"You visited Alexander? Why?"

"Well, I just thought you'd be wanting to know what happened to him after Bull Run and all. The lad doesn't remember being shot, at least not at Bull Run. And no scars, thanks to the bandage I procured for him. And he stopped being scared. He rose to the rank of second lieutenant. Saved lots of men's lives."

"Jasper, that's—I don't know what to say." He was unpredictable, it was true. But he was also thoughtful—more so than she had realized.

"And in a way, Mindy girl, those people owe their lives to you as well. There are advantages to that self-reliance you pride yourself so much on."

Mindy couldn't speak for a moment, as a lump formed in her

throat and her eyes watered. She looked around the room, trying to not to cry.

"Where's Jonathan?" she said. He wasn't in the room with him. Her stomach tightened into a knot. "You didn't send him home without letting me say goodbye, did you?"

"No, no. He's in there." Jasper nodded his head to indicate an open doorway at the far end of the room. "Reading up on his early colonial history in the cyber-archives."

"You . . . *are* going to send him back to his own time eventually, right?" She wanted to say goodbye to the minister properly—the idea of him being stranded permanently in 2512 didn't seem right.

Jasper's brow furrowed. "Well, we've been having a slight problem with that. The chronolyzer's been sampling his blood at fifteen-minute intervals, and his tempose levels are not going down as they should be."

"What does that mean?"

"The chronolyzer finally analyzed his DNA. He's not like other people from 1692. It seems his body's started producing tempose on its own."

Mindy pondered this for a moment. "Maybe that's why Andros seems to like possessing him so much."

"Sure and you're probably right. But we can't send him back to his own time without a way of protecting him from Andros and any Galagians who want to come along and hijack his body."

A beep from the chronolyzer made both of them jump. They looked together at its display.

SUBJECT DNA TEST RESULTS COMPLETE AND FORWARDED TO FREE FASCIST STATE HEADQUARTERS. ORDERS NOW BEING TRANSMITTED FROM THE HIGHEST

LEVELS OF THE FREE FASCIST STATE, MARKED URGENT. STAND BY FOR TRANSMISSION.

The screen went blank, except for the word LOADING . . .

After a moment, a new message appeared. FREE FASCIST STATE DIRECTIVE #25413: IT IS IMPERATIVE TO THE STABILITY OF THE TIME STREAM AND THE FUTURE STATE THAT SUBJECT GOLD AND SUBJECT HARTTHORNE BE KEPT TOGETHER. SUBJECT HARTTHORNE WILL ACCOMPANY YOU BOTH ON YOUR NEXT ASSIGNMENT.

Mindy turned to Jasper in bewilderment. "We have to be kept together? Why? What could we possibly have to do with the stability of the future state?"

Jasper widened his eyes and shook his head, equally bewildered.

"But you can't just yank him out of his own time and keep him in the future!" Mindy's eyes flashed. "He'll go crazy here. All of this futuristic stuff must be blowing his mind as it is. He needs to go back to his own time where he belongs," she hissed, trying not to let her voice carry into the next room.

Suddenly she became aware of the minister's burly frame filling the doorway.

"I'm not so sure that I do, Mindy." The minister's eyes were clouded with worry. "Although the future does 'blow my mind,' as you put it. I've been reading about Salem's history on Jasper's miraculous reading device."

Mindy guessed he was talking about a computer.

"Salem's future is dark indeed," he continued. "Maybe too dark for me to face. So many neighbors dead. So many *friends*. Those are real people to me. And the best efforts by honest men and women to stop the hysteria led only to more death." He paused for a moment, as Mindy and Jasper listened silently. "It's worse than I ever imagined."

An uncomfortable silence hung in the room for a moment. Finally, Mindy spoke up. "But can you really stay in the future, Jonathan? What kind of a life is that?"

The minister shrugged. "I do not know, Mindy. Truly. But as bewildering as the future is, it is fascinating too. Part of me longs to stay here and study these marvels. Part of me wants to learn more of this great nation America. It would seem that the tiny community I grew up in was but a seed—a seed that grew into a vast tree."

Jasper coughed. "Em. Well, I'm glad to hear of your interest, Reverend. You'll be getting to see the birth of that nation firsthand, it would seem." He turned the face of the chronolyzer toward Mindy and Hartthorne.

PREPARE FOR IMMEDIATE TRANSMISSION TO 1775 PHILADELPHIA.

From the chronolyzer's hard drive . . .

Lincoln Log:

5 Little-Known Facts About the Sixteenth President

We all know he was honest. But who was Abe, really?

Fact #1: He helped make his mother's casket

In the fall of 1818, thirty-four-year-old Nancy Hanks Lincoln accidentally drank some toxic cow milk (toxic milk was a danger in the time before pasteurization). She fell seriously ill. Lying on her death bed, she called her children, Sarah, eleven, and Abraham, nine, to her bedside and told them to be good and kind to their father, to each other, and to the world. The children's father, Thomas, a skilled carpenter, made a casket of green pine planks. Abe helped by carving the pegs that held the casket together. The family buried Nancy atop a nearby ridge, without ceremony. Months later, when a traveling clergyman came through that wilderness stretch of southwestern Indiana, near Evansville, he said a funeral prayer over the unmarked grave.

Fact #2: He fought mosquitoes in Illinois

At age twenty-two, Lincoln settled in the tiny village of New Salem, Illinois, and tried to figure out what to do with his life. When Black Hawk, a leader of the allied Sauk and Fox tribes, led a small band of Native American families eastward from Iowa into Illinois with the intent to grow corn there, Lincoln's decision was made. Illinois governor John Reynolds called the migration an invasion and called out the militia, which in turn called for new recruits. Lincoln signed up. In the thoroughly democratic and unruly militia, the likeable Lincoln found himself elected captain of his company. When he first called out the order "Attention!" he was met with a good-natured chorus of "Go to hell!" He never saw battle during his three months of service in the Black Hawk War, but he later recalled "a good many bloody struggles with the mosquitoes."

Fact #3: He didn't always have luck with the ladies

Lincoln was "close friends" with a couple of young lasses of the Illinois persuasion prior to his marriage to Mary Todd. Lincoln's first serious girlfriend caught typhoid and died at age twenty-two, sending Lincoln into a deep depression. The next candidate, Mary Owens, turned the future prez down flat.

Fact #4: He was almost killed by curiosity

With the Civil War in full swing in July 1864, Confederate general Jubal A. Early attacked the Union capital in an attempt to distract Grant, who had Robert E. Lee pinned down in Virginia. The Union forces met Early a short distance from the White House. Lincoln rode out to observe and quickly came under fire. A young officer called out "damned fool!" and told Lincoln to take cover. Some speculate that the young officer in question was Oliver Wendell Homes, Jr., a future supreme court justice, who had such damned fool ideas as sterilizing the mentally ill. As for the failed attack on D.C., Early later said, "We didn't take Washington, but we scared Abe Lincoln like hell."

Fact #5: He dreamed of his own death

It seems Lincoln was a bit of a psychic, although he didn't know it himself. According the account of his friend and bodyguard, Ward Hill Lamon, Lincoln dreamed of hearing someone crying and of himself wandering from empty room to empty room in search of the mourner. In the White House's East Room, he found a covered corpse lying on an ornate funeral platform. Lincoln asked, "Who is dead in the White House?" and someone replied that the corpse was Lincoln's. On the night of April 14, 1865, Lincoln was shot and killed and sent to lie in state on an ornate funeral platform in the White House's East Room.

Number Crunching

17 Civil War Stats

Who says math is too hard? In this list, we really do a number on Civil War history.

4 States with Slavery That Did Not Secede

Delaware, Maryland, Kentucky, and Missouri kept their slaves *and* stayed with the Union during the Civil War. Of course, this didn't always sit well with the citizenry. After Kentucky's state legislature voted not to secede, for example, Kentuckian John Hunt Morgan packed up his militia, the Lexington Rifles, and headed to Confederate Tennessee.

7 States That Formed the Confederate States of America

South Carolina, Mississippi, Florida, Alabama, Georgia, Louisiana, and Texas made up the original CSA in February of 1861. Arkansas, Tennessee, North Carolina, and Virginia joined the rebel alliance in the spring, bringing the total number of Confederate states to eleven before they were brought back into the Union, bloody and beaten.

11 Confederate Dollars a Month Earned by a Confederate Soldier

The worst thing about Confederate Army pay was that it came in the form of Confederate bills, which was about as good as Monopoly money by the end of the war. Because of inflation, the eighteen dollars per month that soldiers drew in 1864 had even less buying power than the eleven dollars per month they received the previous year.

16 U.S. Dollars a Month Earned by a Union Soldier

A Union soldier's pay in 1863 doesn't sound like much, but it was backed by the gold of the U.S. treasury and had many times the buying power of the Confederate dollars.

23 States Solidly Loyal to the Union at the War's Start

Union states stretched from Maine to Pennsylvania in the East, to Minnesota and Iowa in the Midwest, along with the relatively new Pacific Coast states of California and Oregon. During the war, Nevada and Kansas joined the Union as new states, as did a breakaway pro-Union piece of Virginia—as West Virginia.

30 Dollars a Month to Rent a Slave

In 1863 Virginia, a farmer or business owner could pay a monthly rate to a slave's master for the use of the slave. The renter was expected to also house and feed the slave.

47 Survivors of the 1st Minnesota Infantry

On July 2, 1863, the second day of fighting in the three-day Battle of Gettysburg, the 262-man Minnesota regiment attacked a much larger force of Confederates, threatening to break through the Union line. When it was over, 82 percent of the Minnesota First was dead.

50 Dollars for a Bar of Soap

The value of Confederate money declined drastically over the course of the war, as prices correspondingly went up. In 1863, the cost of a barrel of flour reached an unprecedented $100, and by war's end a bar of soap cost $50. Which wasn't so bad, considering that people bathed about once a week back then.

60 Months of War between the States

Between the Confederate attack on Fort Sumter, South Carolina—the opening armed conflict of the war—and Robert E. Lee's surrender at Appomattox, Virginia, almost exactly five years passed.

483 Feet to the Top of the World's Tallest Building

Between 1847 and 1876, the world's tallest building was St. Nilolai's Church, in Hamburg, Germany. The Washington Monument, which sat unfinished during the Civil War, finally reached its height of 555 feet in 1884, the first time that the world's tallest building was in America. The tallest today is Taipei 101, a skyscraper in Taipei, Taiwan. With 101 floors, it stands 1,667 feet.

3,000 Horses Killed in the Battle of Gettysburg

It wasn't just men, of course, who traveled to the verdant fields of Valhalla. Horses were an important part of warfare in the nineteenth century. When facing a cavalry charge, infantrymen often aimed for the horse, a larger target than the rider. On July 3, 1863, Confederate general Isaac Trimble and his horse, Jinny, were wounded with the same bullet. Later that day, Jinny fell dead beneath Trimble as he rode in retreat.

61,122 Civil War-era Washingtonians

In 1680, Washington, D.C., was the United States' fourteenth largest city, and growing fast. The District's population—stimulated in part by the war—more than doubled by 1870, reaching nearly 132,000. Today D.C. ranks twenty-seventh among U.S. cities, with a population of 550,521.

258,000 Confederate Deaths

Many Southern records, likely not very precise anyway, were lost after the war. But historians think more than 32 percent of CSA soldiers died. The rebels also suffered about 225,000 wounded.

359,528 Union Deaths

The victorious North actually lost more soldiers than the South, but the North had a much larger total number of troops enlisted—1,556,000 compared to about 800,000 Confederates. The North also suffered 275,175 wounded.

618,000 Americans Who Died in the Civil War

The estimate is still horrifying today. The Civil War resulted in far more American deaths than any other U.S. conflict. By comparison, about 58,000 American troops were lost in Vietnam. In World War II, the American death toll was 298,000.

813,669 Civil War-era New Yorkers

Today, New York City is home to well over 8 million people. In 1860, New York already was well established as the nation's largest urban community, with a population of 813,669.

31,183,582 Civil War-era Americans

My, how we've grown since 1860. According to the 2000 census, the total U.S. population is greater than 300 million today.

1.4 Billion People (Total!)

1.4 billion people in 1860 sounds like a lot, but by 1927, the world population had reached 2 billion, and by 1974 there were 3 billion of us. Today the number is estimated at 6.5 billion and increasing at a faster rate every day.

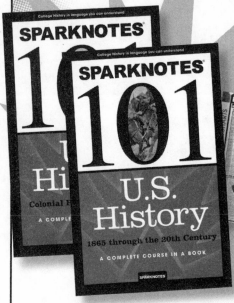